I0520117

Journey
to
Freedom

Also by Karen Lee Field

Books for Young Readers

Land of Miu Series
The Land of Miu
The King's Riddle
The Lion Gods

Cat and Mouse Adventures
House on the Hill

Books for Adults
Domino Effect - A dark novel

A Mini Fantasy Collection

Journey
to
Freedom

Karen Lee Field

First paperback edition 2019

Copyright © Karen Lee Field 2019

"Where Strength Lies" first published in 2008
"Boundaries" first published in 2011

All rights reserved. Except as provided by the
Copyright Act 1968, no part of this publication may be
reproduced, stored in a retrieval system or
transmitted in any form or by any means, electronic
or mechanical, including photocopying and recording,
without the prior written permission of the author.

Published by Karen Lee Field
www.karenleefield.com

ISBN: 978-0-6485959-0-8 (paperback)

Text and cover design by karenleefield.com

For Sandy and Tracy

Having great friends to share my life with
is a gift like no other

.

Index

Where Strength Lies

A sound penetrated Rea's dreams, forcing her awake. Her eyes flew open as she sprang upright on her pallet, the thick furs falling away from her warm body. The night air chilled her skin through the rough, cotton nightgown. What noise had woken her? Was it a fox after the village chickens? Her head tilted from side to side as she listened. All seemed quiet in her mud-brick home. Pulling the furs up over her shoulders, she snuggled back into the warmth.

A scraping sound from overhead made her sit up again. She looked up at the platform where Tad, her five-year-old son, slept. Again, she listened intently. Was he having a restless night? Or worse still, perhaps a nightmare troubled him.

Rea left her bed. Reaching for a shawl, she wrapped it around her shoulders and made her way to the ladder that would take her to her young son.

"Mama?"

Rea froze at the tone of his voice, and she quickly looked up at the platform. Standing near the edge was a heavyset man shroud in darkness, holding Tad firmly by the shoulders.

Rea tried to ignore the pounding of her heart. "Who

are you? What do you want?" she said, keeping her voice even. She moved towards the ladder and placed a foot on the bottom rung.

"Stay where you are," said the man.

His cold tone made Rea obey.

"Please, do not hurt him. He is only a child. We do not have much, but I will give you whatever you need. Food, blankets, anything. Just take it and leave. Please."

"Move back from the ladder," commanded the man.

"Leave him there, he will not do anything," replied Rea. "Neither will I."

"Get back!" The man thrust Tad towards the ladder, but his grip remained firm on the boy's shoulder.

Rea wanted to scream for help, but she would not put Tad in danger. Sudden movements might agitate the stranger. She needed to work out what he wanted. Maybe, once they had descended, she would be able to draw Tad away from him. She moved backwards until a wooden bench stopped her from going any further.

A murmur of voices outside made her glance at the unlatched door. She prayed a neighbour would come to their rescue.

"If you move from that spot or if you make any noise ... I will kill the boy. Understood?" His hands moved to Tad's neck.

Rea's heart missed a beat. "I understand." Fear crawled down her spine.

"Mama," said Tad, his voice small and shaky.

"Everything will be all right." Rea tried to keep her voice soft and reassuring. "Just do as the man says."

The stranger turned to come down the ladder, pulling Tad into the small area between his heavyset body and the wooden rungs. They quickly descended. At the bottom, they turned to face Rea once again. "I am taking the boy," the man announced.

"No!" She rushed forward to grab Tad, but the man swept her to one side. Letting the shawl fall to the floor, Rea turned and slammed her fists repeatedly into the man's chest and clawed at his face. "You cannot have him," she yelled. "Take everything else, but not him."

The back of his hand struck the side of her face. Her head jolted to the side, blood quickly mixed with saliva as she fell onto the hard-packed dirt floor.

"Get out of my way!" He pushed past her, dragging Tad along with him.

"No, I will not let—"

The hut flashed green, and an unexpected force hit Rea in the chest, forcing her flat on her back. Limp, her eyesight wavering, her hearing fuzzy, she could do nothing. Her limbs would not move.

"You killed Mama!"

Not even the distress in Tad's voice could force Rea's body to react. She tried desperately to get up and protect him, but her limbs refused to obey.

She listened to the movements. She heard the door open. Muffled voices outside filled her with hope. A rescue attempt? Hope evaporated, and fear took its place when she heard more unknown voices.

"Burn the place down," the man said with authority. "Be sure the villagers think mother and child died in the fire."

The coldness in the man's voice froze Rea's heart.

Two hooded men appeared. One walked towards the pallet and instantly spoke strange words while the other, much taller than the first, stood beside Rea in silence.

Flames burst up at the edge of Rea's vision. She could smell the furs as they burned. She saw the flames reaching for the platform above. She looked up at the person standing beside her. His hand moved mysteriously. She saw flames envelop her, but felt no heat, no pain. The other man turned and left the hut. Suddenly, the heatless flames engulfing her disappeared, the window shutter above the bench sprung open, and mobility returned to her body. The tall, hooded man helped her to her feet and pointed to the opening. Shock washed over Rea when he helped her up onto the bench. As she climbed through the opening, she heard his footsteps retreat.

"Help!" she yelled as soon as her feet hit the ground. "Somebody help me!"

Her voice echoed in the quiet night. Doors to the huts closest to her home opened. Heads appeared, bleary eyes blinking sleepily.

"Help!" she shouted again. "Strangers are taking Tad."

Seeing the flames and hearing her words, three village men hurried towards her. Other doors opened, and more people wandered out to see what the ruckus was.

"They have taken Tad!" Her voice did not sound like her own. "Help me save him."

Rea and the three village men rounded the hut. Four men in black cloaks were visible. The heavyset man who had taken Tad was dragging him into the back of a cart, while two other men stood guard. The fourth man stood further away, nearer to the burning hut. Rea reasoned that this must be the one who had spared her life.

"Stop them!" said Rea as she ran towards the cart.

"Hey, what are you doing with the boy?" one of the village men yelled.

"Let him go," yelled another.

Behind her, Rea heard more villagers arrive. Her hopes soared. She knew the villagers would do whatever it took to help get Tad back.

The village men headed straight for the cloaked figures standing at the back of the cart. Rea ran towards the side, nearer to her terrified son. Tad's eyes, as round as the moon, held her gaze, pleading for her to take him away from the stranger standing over him.

At the cart, Rea did not hesitate; she grabbed hold of the side and pulled herself inside. Lifting her gaze, the hooded man who had helped her before came into view. His face still hidden, she stared at him for a split second, an uneasy feeling clutching at her belly. She attempted to stand up. The heavyset man grabbed her by the shoulders and tried to shove her over the side. Rea stumbled but grabbed the man's cloak to stop herself from falling out. Closing her fist, she put all her weight behind it as she slammed it into the man's groin. He sank to his knees, his eyes rolling upwards in pain.

Rea grabbed Tad, but before she was able to move, a rough hand gripped her wrist and twisted her in a half-circle. As Tad dropped into the cart with a bang and started to cry, Rea's gaze found the hooded man once again. Who was he? What was he doing?

A low growl escaped the man who held her. The pressure on her wrist increased. Pain shot up her arm. Rea fell to her knees in front of him, realising he intended to break the bone.

The hooded man made strange hand movements. Instinctively, she pulled away from the blow she expected from her assailant, but none came. Suddenly the pressure on her arm ceased. The bulky stranger fell backwards with a groan. Rea spun around. She did not know what had happened, but she knew the hooded man had saved her again. Why? Did he have other plans for her son?

There was no time to figure it out. Rea turned, lifted Tad over the side of the cart and lowered him to the ground. She jumped over the side herself, got to her feet and with one glance at the hooded stranger, she snatched up Tad's small frame and ran. She ran from the village, the people gathered around her burning hut and the strangers in cloaks who intended to take her precious child.

She ran across a clearing that would take her and her son into the forest. The noise and yells behind her pushed her on. She heard one of the strangers cursing her profusely. The trees lit up in a green shimmer.

"Do not harm the boy!" yelled the leader. "He has the Gift."

Puffing, Rea reached the tree line. The immediate area suddenly lit up around them in an assortment of vivid colour. She lowered Tad to the ground and took hold of his hand. A loud explosion sounded behind them. Screams filled the night.

"Mama?"

She tugged at Tad's hand. "Run!"

Within the canopy of the trees, filtered moonlight lit their way. On the horizon, Rea saw the sky slowly changing colour. Morning would soon spill over onto the cold, damp earth.

She had used the narrow path often, so she was sure-footed. They moved deeper into the forest. Why had they come for her son? What had the stranger meant when he said Tad had *the Gift*? More importantly, where could she take Tad to escape? The question seemed to push all other thought aside.

From a distance, screams continued to drift through the night. Would the strangers follow her? Before the thought had fully formed, she heard deep voices. They were closer than before. They wanted Tad. She would ensure they did not get him!

Think. Maybe the men would assume she would continue to use the path and make her way to the next village. She instantly veered to her right, taking Tad directly into the trees. If she could find somewhere to hide, she would be able to focus, and maybe then she could outsmart them.

"Mama, I am tired."

Slowing her pace a little, Rea looked down at her son. He breathed in short, shallow gasps. What a fool she was to think that his small body could keep pace with her long legs. Scooping him up into her arms, she continued at a half run, half walk—the first rays of sunlight drying the night dew.

"They went this way." The voice echoed clearly through the trees.

Rea tried to move faster, but Tad's weight slowed her down.

"Are we going to the Falls?" asked Tad, grasping her neck tightly.

The Falls. What a good idea! She kissed his soft cheek and changed direction again.

The ground sloped upwards. Rea felt pain developing in her side. She lowered Tad to the ground. "I cannot carry you any longer."

"I can walk, Mama," he said, smiling up at her.

"Good boy," said Rea, squeezing his hand.

Hand in hand, they climbed the slope. It gradually grew steeper and steeper until they had to use their hands to pull themselves up. The physical exertion, and warm morning sun, quickly had them sweating profusely.

The sound of water spilling over the Falls replaced the murmur of voices behind them. The ground levelled. Rea smiled reassuringly at Tad, despite the apprehension gripping her stomach.

Without warning, a hand clamped over her mouth. Rea struggled, but her captor was strong and quickly dragged her into the undergrowth. She heard Tad crying. He called to her, but the sound ended as soon as it had begun.

What had happened to him?

She swung her arms wildly and kicked her legs, but to no avail. In desperation, she managed to catch the man's flesh between her teeth. She heard him grunt, but his hand remained firmly over her mouth.

He pulled her to the ground before whispering in her ear. "Quiet! I am trying to help you."

Rea's heart jumped. Her teeth instantly let go, and she allowed herself to be restrained.

"Your son is with us and is safe. The others are coming," he said. "They must not see or hear us."

Rea looked over the top of the hand holding her, through the long grass and shrub, and watched two men amble past. Their demeanour told her they were exhausted after the long climb up the hill.

"Damn fool," one of them said. "We should have finished her when we had the chance."

"You are the fool." Rea recognised the voice of the man who had taken Tad. "She was carrying the boy, we would have killed him too, and King Calo wants him alive."

"Where are the others?"

"They went another—"

The voices faded as they proceeded towards the noise of The Falls. The hand over Rea's mouth relaxed. Now she could attempt to escape, but the rational part of her brain told her to wait. If this man meant them harm, they would not be hiding.

"I can lead you to safety," he said as he removed his hand from her face.

Rea sat straight-backed and rigid, her mind taking in his voice and the softness in his tone. It reminded her of something long past. She wanted to listen to him say more, so that the pieces of the puzzle might fall together.

"If you scream, they will come back," he continued. "I do not want that, and I know you do not either." He stood and looked in the direction the other men had gone. "We must go."

"Who are you?" Rea rose, one hand automatically reaching out for Tad. "Why are you helping us?"

"You do not know?"

Rea tried to glimpse his face, but she only saw the glint of an eye. Before she could respond to his question, he spoke again.

"Strangely, Rea, I thought you would." He scooped Tad into his arms.

He knows my name! Shock and panic flooded through her body, and she shook her head in confusion. "Please, give him to me."

"It will be faster if I carry him. He is safe with me." He

turned and quickly walked in the opposite direction to the men. "Trust me."

He held her son, so she followed, but a tiny niggling voice inside her head told her she had missed a clue. Her gaze never left his black-caped back. Could she trust him? Her mind told her to grab Tad and run. Her heart told her she would be stupid to give in to fear and uncertainty when all the evidence proved he was on their side.

Before long, she found the terrain had changed. Instead of soft grass padding her sore feet, she now walked on stone. He led her into a cave. She stopped and stared into the pitch blackness. She felt a hand on her shoulder, and then Tad was transferred into her arms. Closing her eyes, she buried her face into his hair and hugged him close.

"Wait here. I need to conceal the entrance."

Rea jumped when a soft white light lit up the cave. She stared at the solid stone in front of her and spun around. The tall man stood with his arms held high, his fingers curled as if he meant to claw the eyes out of any person who dared go near him. The light travelled away from his hands and shimmered in the entrance of the cave. The opening snapped shut, leaving them trapped within walls of stone.

Rea's hands went clammy and her throat dry. Suddenly regretting her decision to follow this hooded stranger, she swallowed and took several steps away from him. "What are you doing?" she whispered, unable to keep the terror from her voice. "You tricked us."

The white shimmering evaporated, and the cave returned to blackness.

"No. I ... wait, we need light."

Again, something about his voice tugged at her heart.

Blue light lit the cave. Rea turned in a semi-circle and gasped at the blue glow in the man's hand in disbelief. Tad reached out, but she quickly grabbed his small hand and held it firmly within her own.

"We are safe for now. I have cast a glamour spell over the entrance. From the outside, it looks like solid rock. The spell will also change the noise we make. No one will know we are here. It will give us time to talk."

Rea looked around the cave, confirming once again that solid rock surrounded them. There was no escape. The only sound was her heartbeat drumming loudly in her ears. "Who are you? What do you want with us?" she asked again, her voice sounding shrill.

Finally, the man reached up and pulled off his hood.

Rea gasped and felt her mouth fall open. "Heb!"

Sapphire blue eyes gleamed at her. She held her breath as her gaze took in the mass of dark hair which fell in a mess around his tanned face. Breathing out slowly, she fought against the impulse to lean forward and let her fingertip run along the masculine jaw that had not seen the sharp edge of a blade in some days. Her gaze took in the dimpled smile that showed his brilliant white teeth. All these things, except the colour of his hair, had been inherited by their son. She could not take her eyes off Heb's face. She was unable to speak. Finally, she forced herself to take a breath and look away.

Without warning, anger surged through her body. She had once loved this man with all her heart, but he had walked away without a word. Not knowing what had happened, she had fretted for him, imagining all sorts of terrible things which might account for his disappearance. Finally, a single rumour had crushed her. Someone had seen him in the city with another woman. Then she had discovered she was with child. Now, he dared to walk back into her life. Did he have any idea how much he had hurt her?

She rushed towards him. She wanted to inflict pain, but his quick response stopped even that satisfaction. He grabbed her hand before it slapped his face and held it firmly between them.

"I am sorry, Rea." His voice croaked. "Please, let me explain."

She swallowed the sob in her throat. She would not show weakness. Not to him. She snatched her hand out of his grasp and turned away. She walked to where the cave's entrance should have been and placed one hand on the rock. "How did you do this? What are you?"

She felt a presence at her side and looked down to find Tad holding tightly onto her nightgown. Rea followed his fascinated gaze and found Heb smiling down at Tad with sparkling eyes. Rea felt her heart surge.

"I am a mage. I have magical abilities," replied Heb.

"Mage? Magical abilities?" Rea shook her head. "But that cannot be true. I mean ... I have heard rumours about such things, but I thought they were just pensive notions of a bored mind, nothing more."

"I do not know what rumours you have heard, but I can assure you that magic runs in the veins of some people." He reached out and pushed a strand of hair from her face.

Rea's heartbeat raced, but she stepped away from him. "What has that got to do with us?"

Heb looked meaningfully at Tad.

Rea gasped. "No," she said, shaking her head. "He is not!"

"He is," replied Heb. "It runs in families, and that is why the king knows who to watch. He is unaware of my connection with Tad, but the village storyteller has been reporting to the king for some years—"

"What? But she is a friend!"

"She is also a mother, and it was the only way she could save her son. The king spared him, but she had to report any suspicions she had about the other children. Do not think badly of her. She did what she had to do. If she did not, then they would have returned for *her* son."

"I cannot believe it," said Rea, feeling nauseous.

"Tad did something unusual six months ago, which she witnessed. She has been making regular reports to the castle ever since."

Rea stared at her son. As his mother, surely she would know if Heb's claim was valid. A mother knew her little boy better than anyone.

Heb took a small, cloth-wrapped parcel from inside his cloak and handed it to Tad. "Are you hungry? There are strips of dried meat and some nuts in there."

Tad took the parcel and smiled. "Thank you."

Rea and Heb watched their son sit down and carefully open the cloth to reveal the food.

"Sit down, Rea," said Heb. "Let me tell you what I know."

She did not move.

"This is my first mustering," he continued quickly. "It was the only way I could get close enough to help you."

"Mustering? What do you mean? What about the other woman?"

"The other woman?" He paused, frowning. "Oh, the

rumour. It is not true."

Frustrated, she tutted. "Right, tell me what is true." She sat on the ground, pulled Tad onto her lap and looked up at Heb. "I am listening."

"Thank you," he said, his eyes not leaving hers. He lowered himself onto the ground opposite her.

"First, I want to know why you stopped coming to see me?" asked Rea, looking into his bright blue eyes.

Sadness washed over Heb's face, his shoulders slumped forward, and he stared at the dirt between them.

"People disappear or have accidents when they have the Gift. Or that is what the king likes everyone to believe. What you believe about me is a fabricated lie. I did not walk away, Rea. There was never another woman. I intended to ask for your hand in the spring. You were my world." Long fingers gently touched hers. "I love you."

Rea refused to respond. "What happened then?"

"Without warning, the mages came one night and took me away," replied Heb. "Back then, King Calo was careful not to give away his secrets."

"And you think he is giving them away now?" She heard the sarcasm in her voice. "I do not seem to know what is going on."

Heb nodded, his face grim. "I know, but before long everyone will know what his plans are. Even after all she has done to prevent it, they will still take the storyteller's son."

Despite everything, Rea felt sorry for the woman. "Tell me. What are the king's plans?"

"He intends to use warrior mages against the king of Docsii in the north."

Heb fell silent, and Rea stared at his profile. She saw remnants of an old scar running the length of his face. It started on his forehead, stopped at his eyebrow, and continued just below the eye. She cringed as she realised how lucky he had been. The jagged line ran at an angle across his cheekbone towards the soft skin where his jaw started. Rea then noticed the difference in skin thickness around his neck. What had happened to cause such a scar? Finally, she realised that she had not recognised his voice because of this injury. He had changed a lot in the five or so years since she had last seen him, but she still glimpsed the man she fell in love with. Without realising what she was doing, she turned her hand over and let her fingers entwine with his. "Go on," she said, her voice softening as she became aware of the heat tingling through her body.

"I was taken to the castle, where the mages tested me. The tests are designed to find out if I had magical ability. They did not care about anything else. What they did could have killed me, but they did not care about that, because if I did not show ability, they would have killed me anyway."

He looked up at the sound of her gasp, and his eyes narrowed. "I saw them kill others—men and small boys, even a woman once, who knew nothing about what was going on." His gaze rested on Tad.

Something pulled at her heart as she watched Heb's hand reach out and gently touch Tad's face.

Tad recoiled. He turned to face Rea and nestled against her. Her arms automatically went around him protectively, but she saw the look on Heb's face. She saw the hurt and rejection, and she felt her throat restrict in anguish.

"Tad, it is all right," said Rea, smoothing his hair. "This is your papa. He would never hurt you."

Without moving, Tad strained to look at Heb's face.

A moment of silence followed.

Rea shifted her position so that her son had a clear view of his father. "Finish your story," she said to Heb.

Heb glanced at Tad before continuing. "The tests proved I had the ability they were looking for, so they put me to training, along with a couple of others. For a year, we were well guarded. Escape was not an option as it would result in torture. They did not want to kill us. They wanted to break and bend us to their will. They had other means of making us do what they wanted." His hand touched the rough skin on his neck. "One by one, we succumbed to their wishes.

"I thought about you every night. Then one morning, we were herded into a cart and taken to the city. We travelled through the village. I saw you. You were holding a baby, and I knew it was mine."

Rea nodded. Only a fool would not see the likeness.

"I knew that if I had the magical ability, then Tad might have it also. That is why I stayed away from you when I finally had the trust of the mages and could leave the castle whenever I wished. I did not want to alert them to Tad. I did not want them to snatch him away from you as they had me. I refused to allow them to test him." He let the sentence hang in the air between them for a moment. "I thought that if I stayed away, then Tad would be safe."

Rea knew in her heart that Heb had done what he thought was best for all of them at the time.

"Six months ago," he continued, "I learned that a boy in your village had the ability. They said he was not yet five and they would wait until a few months after his birthday before taking and testing him. They said his name was Tad."

A chill crept along every bone in Rea's body. She pressed her lips to the top of Tad's blond head and held him tight.

"The news troubled me, so I left the castle and went to the village. I made some inquiries, and that is when I knew for sure that they meant to test my son."

Rea's heart raced. "You should have warned me then. I could have taken Tad and gone away."

Heb shook his head. "I immediately started to plan our escape. I knew that we would be fighting against the best mages imaginable, and they would not rest until they had him in their grasp. I had to find a way to conquer them."

Our escape. Rea smiled.

Heb leaned forward and reached out to cup her face in his right hand. His thumb traced her cheekbone before touching her lips. Tingles rushed up and down her spine. His hand moved into her long hair. She shivered at his gentle caress and then he pulled her head towards him. Rea, still cradling Tad in her arms, held her breath. Heb's lips found hers. Gentle. Loving. He barely breathed, but his hold soon became firm and urgent, washing all her doubts away. She reached up and touched his face. A guttural sound escaped him, and then he released her.

"I have always loved you, Rea," he said, his voice low. "And I will not allow them to test Tad."

"How can we escape?"

"I figure the only way to beat magicians is to use illusion."

The ground beneath them rumbled. Dust sprinkled over them from above. They heard nothing, but sunlight shone through the entrance once again.

"What happened?" asked Rea.

"They must have used a reversal incantation to break the glamour spell. It is performed at a distance, especially if the caster is unsure which spell was conjured. It proves they do not know where we are but suspect you are hidden by magic." Heb rose to his feet, lifted Tad into his arms and grabbed Rea's hand.

She allowed herself to be dragged out of the cave and through the trees yet again.

For a while, Heb led them downhill, backtracking. Rea grew increasingly nervous as they headed closer to the village. Then she realised they had changed direction and were heading away from the village. The knot in her stomach loosened, but the muscles in her legs tightened as the ground steepened.

A mage, the end of his black cloak fluttering in the gentle breeze, stepped out in front of them. "You found them, Heb." He pulled his hood back to reveal his face.

"Ragon?" Rea gasped. "But I thought you had been killed in a hunting accident?"

A sneer twisted Ragon's face. "Not all accidents are what they seem, Rea. Yours would have been convincing if we did not have a traitor within our midst."

"Ragon, we do not want trouble. Just let us pass," said Heb.

Ragon's eyes narrowed. "Sorry, I cannot let you or the boy escape."

Heb turned, his body shielding Tad from danger. With a wave of his arm, Heb produced a sizzling white light in the palm of his hand, which he quickly threw in the direction of the surprised mage. The ball of light shot through the air between them, striking the man firmly in the chest before lifting him off his feet and throwing him back into the trees. Rea watched as the man landed heavily with a grunt.

"Come, Rea," Heb called over his shoulder as he ran past Ragon.

Ragon rubbed his chest and placed a hand on the ground attempting to get to his feet. Rea quickly followed Heb.

They had not gone far when they heard Ragon yelling behind them. "Over here! Heb is helping them escape."

The trees thinned out, allowing the sun's hot rays to beat down on them. Panting, Rea pushed herself on, trying to catch up with Heb and Tad. She saw another mage before he stepped out in front of them. She opened her mouth to warn Heb, but it was already too late. The man faced Heb, his dark eyes glaring at them.

"Heb, this is treason," said the mage.

"My family is more important than the king and his war," replied Heb. "I do not want to hurt you, Zarf, but I will if I have to."

"You are a fool if you think we will let you leave with the boy," said Zarf. "You are a powerful mage, and the boy may have inherited your ability. The king needs you both."

Rea continued to walk up behind them, listening intently to their conversation.

"Would you let them test your child?" asked Heb.

"My daughter is dead. The king—"

Rea felt the presence behind her a split-second before a hand closed over her mouth, but there was no time to react. Ragon pulled her back against his body. She felt his breath hot against her cheek, and a foul stench filled her nose and mouth. "Do as we command and you will survive the day."

She tried to force a scream from her throat, but his hand muffled the sound. She struggled. His grip tightened. Pain shot down her arms as his fingertips dug into her flesh.

Then she heard yelling, and her focus found Tad reaching for her over his father's shoulder. "Mama?"

Heb turned. She saw anger wash over his face. He moved towards her, but something forced him backwards. He fell, and Tad scrambled out of his arms and stood up. Large tears fell down his pale cheeks.

Struggling against Ragon, Rea twisted and turned. She scratched and tried to bite, kicked and elbowed. Tad called for her the entire time, but she could not free herself.

Ragon cursed her. His hands found her throat. She went limp for a moment, unable to breathe. Images flashed through her mind—running through shallow water laughing, as a child, her face glowing with happiness. Her mother sitting with her at bedtime to tell her stories and kiss her goodnight. Stretching out on the pallet in her hut one hot summer's night watching Heb dream. The midwife placing her newborn son on her naked belly.

Tad needed her. Heb had declared his love for her. She was not ready to die.

She opened her eyes and saw a white ball of light sitting on Tad's palm. He stared at it. Rea drove her elbow into Ragon's stomach and let the force push her fist up and over her shoulder into his face. With a grunt, he let her go, and she fell to the ground. Tad's spell collided with the mage, throwing him against the nearest tree.

Rea sprang to her feet, rubbing her neck and still gulping in air. Grabbing a fallen branch, she swung it hard and hit Ragon squarely on the shoulder. The splintering sound confirmed broken bones.

"Rea?"

She turned to find Heb and Tad running towards her, leaving Zarf spread-eagled on the ground behind them. She dropped her weapon when Heb released Tad's hand and pulled her to him. Her arms went around him, and they clung to each other for only a moment.

"I am so proud of you," breathed Heb. "Quickly, we have to keep moving."

"Where?"

"There's no time to explain." Picking Tad up again, he continued on his way.

The trees parted, and the smell of the ocean filled Rea's nostrils. Leaving the slope behind them, she discovered tall grass that seemed to roll gently into the sky. Rea stared ahead of her, watching the grass move with the breeze, knowing that at some point the grass ended at a cliff's edge.

Panic set in. "Heb, there is no escape from here. We have to turn back."

"No," he said, looking from her face to Tad's. "This is our destination. Our only way to freedom."

Rea stopped walking. "If we go any further, we will be trapped."

"They know Tad has the ability. Without any training, he produced a spell after seeing me cast it once. It takes some mages months of practice to do that. And he did it without having to verbalise the spell. He's a Soma Mage

29

like me, and that makes him powerful. They will never let him leave. They will hunt us both wherever we go. We will never be free. This is the only way."

"But, Heb—"

"I have thought about this long and hard, Rea. Trust me."

"Heb, you should have told us he is your son," a strained voice called from behind them.

Rea and Heb spun around.

Using a tree branch for support, the man who had taken Tad from the hut came along a different path towards them. He stopped, leaning heavily on the tree branch. He puffed and panted with exhaustion. Zarf stood on the other track, and walking up behind him was Ragon.

"Would that have made a difference, Embri?" asked Heb.

Embri threw back his head and laughed.

"Ignore him," Heb said to Rea. "He does not want to kill us. Keep walking."

"You cannot escape," said Embri, his voice almost taunting.

Rea felt Heb's hand on her arm. He positioned her so that he was between her and the mages. She knew he was trying to protect her. The mages did not want to kill Heb or Tad, but her life meant nothing to them.

"Heb!" Embri's voice sounded a little desperate now.

"Keep walking," said Heb. "The more distance between them and us, the better."

"Incendia!" The strange word echoed in the breeze.

Rea groaned as Heb pushed her roughly to the ground.

"Keep down," he said.

When she looked up, she saw him standing with his feet apart. Between his outstretched hands glowed a transparent shield which sucked the life out of the fireballs hurled at them.

"Help me," screamed Embri to the mages beside him.

Zarf lifted his hand. "Incendia."

Rea jolted at the sight of the fireball that appeared in his hand. She reached for Tad and, pulling him towards her, covered his body protectively with hers.

She stared at the mages. Ragon could not conjure a fireball or anything else for that matter, and he returned to nursing his limp arm instead. When her gaze returned to Heb, without him uttering a word, she saw the shield transform until it was double its original size. Heb held it with two hands now, but she also noticed the beads of sweat forming on his temple. How much longer would he be able to produce this protection?

"Get up, Rea," said Heb, his voice strained. "We have to run."

Taking Tad's hand, Rea rose and starting running. There was no sign of the shield's protection any longer. Fireballs whizzed past them, landing in the grass around them. Some smouldered for a moment before dying, while others caught the grass alight and started small fires.

"Incendia Parietis," yelled Zarf. No fireball followed, but an explosion of flame to Rea's right forced her to change course.

"This way," said Heb, who snatched Tad up from the ground and continued to run.

Rea ran as fast as she could. More fireballs exploded around them, but Heb pushed her in another direction until the flames were behind them.

"Do not stop," said Heb.

She listened to his boots thump on the ground behind her, finding comfort in the thought he was nearby.

"Interimo!" Rea recognised Embri's voice.

The cliff's edge was not far, but where to go from there, she did not know.

"Mama!"

Rea whirled around in time to see Heb and Tad rising from the ground. As she stood paralysed to the spot, they turned to face their enemy. A sizzling white ball of light sat on Tad's palm, a black haze on Heb's. Together they cast their spells. Heb seemed surprised to see the white ball of light follow his blackness. He looked down at his son and bent to pick him up.

Behind the roaring flames that had cut them off from their prey, the three mages looked shocked as the black and white balls merged and struck Embri in the chest. Embri fell to the ground, and Zarf and Ragon rushed to his side. The yells that followed were washed away by shock as Rea noticed Heb staggering towards her, Tad held tightly in one arm. A moment later, Heb fell to the ground too.

"No!" Rea ran towards them.

As she got closer, she heard the murmur of Heb's voice as he spoke with Tad.

"I can remember that," Tad replied, tears rolling down his face.

At Heb's side, Rea sank to her knees. "Heb, get up."

Tad climbed to his feet. "Papa?"

"Do not forget what I said, Tad. It is important." Heb's gaze never left Tad's face. A smile touched his lips. "I am so proud, my son."

Rea grabbed Heb's shoulder. "What happened? Get up. The flames will not hold them back for long. We have to keep moving."

"I cannot," said Heb. "Embri used the killing curse on me. I suppose he thought to have one of us is better than none. He would never trust me again, but Tad can be conditioned."

"But ..." Rea looked over her shoulder. The flames were beginning to die down.

"Embri is dead," said Heb. "Our spells combined killed him instantly."

"There is no time for this. Get up." Tears stung her eyes. Her fingers touched his hair, running the length of his face.

Heb reached for her hand and squeezed it. "Go."

"No! I will not leave you." She lifted his hand to her lips and kissed it.

Heb lifted his other hand and pointed behind her. "Go ... to the cliff. Tad must touch ... the boulder ... as you pass. Tad ... will activate ..." his eyes fluttered closed.

"Heb!" Rea grabbed his face in her hands and kissed him. "You cannot die. I love you."

His eyes slowly opened. He smiled weakly. "Jump."

Rea shook her head. Tears spilled down her face. "Jump? Are you crazy? Please get up. We can escape."

"Trust me, Rea."

His eyes closed again.

"Heb?" she cried, sobs of anguish shaking her body.

His fingers reached for hers. "Must have boulder on left ... Tad must touch ..." his voice no more than a whisper, "jump ... go in cave ... throw the sacks ... trust me ... save our son."

His fingers let go of her, and his hand fell lifeless to

the ground.

"No!" Rea hunched over Heb's body and sobbed.

"Mama, the men are coming," said Tad.

Her son's tiny voice pushed through the grief. She looked up and through blurry vision saw Ragon and Zarf weaving their way through the now dying flames.

Trust me.

Her finger traced the strong jaw bone of Heb's face. "I do."

Rea rose, grabbed Tad's hand, and they ran. The sea breeze gushed through her hair, and her breath came in short gasps.

"Where is ... the ... boulder?"

"There." Tad pointed.

Rea scooped Tad up into her arms. Holding him firmly against her thumping heart, she ran as fast as she could.

"Give us the boy, and we will let you live," yelled Ragon.

Rea ran on. She could already hear the raging water below the cliff.

"No one else need die," said Zarf. "Just give us the boy."

Trust me.

Pain gripped her side, and her arms ached from Tad's weight, but she staggered on.

The boulder to her immediate left, Rea stopped. "Touch the boulder, Tad."

Tad obeyed, and she swung around to face her assailants.

"You have nowhere to go," said Zarf. "Give us the boy."

Trust me. Save our son.

"No, I will never hand him over. Never!"

Rea saw the look of confusion on Zarf's face and then the undeniable look of disbelief. As he took a step forward, Rea turned and jumped off the cliff.

They landed with a thump. Groaning, Rea looked up and saw they had only dropped six feet. She turned and looked over her shoulder and saw an entrance to a cave. Heb's words now made sense. Pushing Tad towards the opening, she said, "Find the sacks and hand them to me. Be quick."

"Sacks?"

"Just look for them, Tad," she scurried off the wooden platform, her gaze following a length of rope. "Quickly!"

"Is this it?"

Rea looked at Tad. In one hand, he held up a stuffed sack stitched together to look like a person. Around its neck hung a black cape, much like the one Heb wore. "Are there others?"

Tad nodded.

"Bring me the other two."

Tad turned and grabbed two other sack people. One, with straw sewn to its head, was much shorter than the other. The taller of the two had a tattered dress pulled over it. She looked down at her nightgown and wondered if they would be able to tell the difference.

Rea snatched them from Tad and stepped out onto the wooden platform. The smell of the ocean swept over her. Voices filtered down to them. The mages were almost at the cliff's edge now.

Rea threw the dummies and watched them land on the jagged rocks far below. She peered over the edge for a fraction of a second and her heart missed a beat—a mother and child lay dead on the rocks, she could have sworn it was real and then she remembered the glamour spell.

She stepped back off the platform and pulled on the rope. The platform rose until it rested against the opening. Sunlight struggled through the narrow slits between the boards of the platform, providing very little light.

Rea sank to the ground, still gripping the rope, but already the wooden platform had merged with the rock. Heb had thought of everything.

"Mama?"

"I am here, Tad." She pulled her son towards her and hugged him close.

"I am scared."

"Shh."

"She jumped to her death," Ragon's voice floated down to them. "See, their twisted bodies are down there, on the rocks."

"What a fool!" said Zarf.

"She took her son to his death too."

There was a brief silence.

"Should we retrieve the bodies?"

"No, the ocean will take care of them," said Zarf. "We have wasted enough time on them. Come, we have another young mage to muster and train."

"But none as powerful as the boy. She was crazy to jump—"

The voices faded away, leaving Rea and Tad sitting in the scratchy dimness of the cave, too scared to move. They sat huddled together for a long time before Rea stirred. Dazed, she felt as if she was waking from a horrible dream. "Tad, what else is here? Did you see a lantern?"

A moment later, a blue light, held in the palm of Tad's hand, lit up the cave. Rea stared at the light in surprise.

"It is not hot, Mama." He paused. "Papa told me a special word to use when I touched the boulder."

"I did not hear you speak," replied Rea.

"He said the word is more powerful when you say it inside your mind. Lots of words are."

Rea stared at her young son's face in shock. "So that is what Heb meant. You activated the spell."

She pushed strands of blond hair out of his face and looked at the blue light in his hand. "How long have you been able to do that?"

"A long time ..." his voice faded as he stared at the figure sitting beside the wooden platform. "It looks like Papa."

"I know." A lump formed in Rea's throat. "He planned for us all to escape together."

"But ..." tears spilled down Tad's face.

"But now we will go on alone." Rea spotted a pack and knew that everything she needed would be inside. Propped up on top of three brown cloaks and a pile of clothes, beside the pack, was a lantern. On the stone wall opposite them, Heb had written in charcoal, "Go down the tunnel. Exit through woods. Go south to safety."

He had planned every detail of their escape, including a backup plan.

Rea reached for her son and pulled him close to her. She would never allow anyone to threaten his life again. Tears dropped onto his blond hair as she held him tight. Heb had loved Tad, without even knowing him.

Everything he had done, he had done for them. His only desire was to keep his family secure and to take them to safety. He had used illusion to free them, and she would use trust to keep them safe.

"We will eat now and then we will sleep until nightfall," she told Tad.

The coming of the new dawn would find them far from the cave's entrance, heading south.

Madla's Quest

The raconteur was short, with a hooked nose and a crop of wild grey hair topped with a quilted hat. His rotund belly evidenced many meals over recent moons, yet his jacket and leggings were patched in multiple places, especially the elbows and knees. Everything about the man looked mismatched and strange.

Yet the sparkle in his eyes and the words he spoke captivated his audience. Apart from his mysterious voice, utter silence claimed the great hall.

"Genard froze in horror. He felt the presence of something terrible standing behind him. It was dark, and he was scared ... his sword wavered ... he turned and looked into small, red eyes."

Candlelight danced across the walls. Standing in the centre of the chamber, the storyteller neared the end of his story.

"The young man swallowed and took a step backwards. His throat tightened, and sweat covered his aching body. He was tired and wanted nothing more than for the night to be over. After everything he had seen and fought that long night, this was the worst. The beast lifted its head and flames shot from its gaping jaws."

The audience gasped. The storyteller pushed his tall, quilted hat back and jumped up onto the closest tabletop. He stared at the faces around him as the crowd stirred anxiously.

"Genard fell to the ground, but he was lucky because the beast did not want to kill him—not yet!"

"He struggled to his feet, but there was nowhere to go—" The storyteller grabbed a tall candlestick from the table. The candle fell to the wooden surface, an ominous thud in the stillness, but no one watched the flame extinguish. All eyes stared at the storyteller as he twirled on his heel and thrust the sword into the empty air, before stepping back ready to strike again. "—except towards the dragon," he continued. "Genard took one step and then another. His heart pounded in his weary chest."

Several of the audience leaned forward in their chairs.

"The dragon reared onto its hind legs and spread its wings. More flames gushed from the dragon's mouth. This time the furniture caught alight. Flames flared up around him. Finally, Genard had light to see by."

The man swung around to face the people on the other side of the hall. Several of them yelped with fright at the sudden movement. "The dragon was huge," the storyteller roared, his eyes wide. "Genard was terrified but knew this was the moment to act. He darted forward," the storyteller ran along the tabletop and thrust his sword into the invisible dragon, "and the sword disappeared into the dragon's flesh. Blood gushed from the wound, but Genard did not dither; he freed the sword and thrust it again. Deeper. Harder."

Women sat in horror; their faces hidden in their hands, while the men leaned forward, eager to hear more.

"Flames continued to stream from the dragon's jaws. Genard intended to thrust his sword one final, triumphant time, but before it pierced the thick hide of the dragon, a mighty kick sent him flying backwards. Covered in blood, everything burning around him, Genard knew this was his last chance to escape."

The storyteller fell silent. He dropped the candlestick, and it clattered onto the table. Several women screamed. He waited for the hall to fall silent again.

"On his hands and knees, Genard crawled in the direction of the exit," the storyteller whispered. He jumped from the tabletop and grabbed a man by the shoulder. Now, he acted the part of the dragon. "The dragon flipped Genard over. Red eyes burned into his. Genard knew then that this was to be his death day. The dragon slashed Genard's throat an instant later." He slashed at the man's throat with the tip of his finger then turned away.

"Genard died. But the dragon will return another day to fight again."

The banquet hall was silent. Not daring to move or speak, the people stared at the short man with the quilted hat and the hooked-nose. The storyteller smiled and turned to face the master of the castle—Lord Tyalt.

"My lord, I have delivered my story, and as payment, I request a meal as promised," the storyteller announced. "Have you not been entertained? And has there ever been such a silence in the great hall after such a magnificent story? You seem surprised, my lord."

Lord Tyalt sat perfectly still for a moment. He looked

around the hall, before turning his gaze back to the storyteller. "Your story was indeed unique."

The storyteller smiled and bowed. "It was based on truth, my lord. On another occasion, the story might be quite different."

A smile appeared on Lord Tyalt's face. "Yes, quite different. You delivered on your promise." He signalled to the servants to bring in the food. "Be seated, storyteller. You have earned the right to eat at my tables."

Noise gradually filled the banquet hall.

Madla had never served at tables before. Since the tender age of fourteen, the highlight of her day was washing dishes. As a scullery maid in a grand castle, the dishes seemed never-ending. Hundreds of them. Every day. Every single day for ten long years.

Madla hated washing dishes.

To be offered the chance to serve tables in the great hall was an opportunity Madla did not intend to let pass. Already she had witnessed her first storytelling, and it was brilliant. She could not wait to tell Silva, her best friend. What would happen next?

"Get to work!"

Madla snapped out of her daydream and set about taking endless plates of food to the tables. It was much harder than she thought. Lord Tyalt enjoyed entertaining a lot of people, and the great hall was often festive, loud and packed with guests. This night was no exception. She hurried back and forth between the kitchen and the great hall, trying to avoid the crude remarks of the men and the open glares of the women.

By the time everyone had a plate in front of them, the meals were already growing cold.

Within the hour, her long, grey gown was splattered with gravy, the white-linen cloth she held was filthy from wiping spilled ale off the tables, and she'd had more men smack her backside than she liked to count. She was exhausted, and her bosom heaved in her low-cut gown as she wondered if serving tables was any better than washing dishes. Maybe she needed to set her sights higher.

Why was she a lowly servant, when she could be like one of the women seated at the tables? She would have a lord at her side and pretty gowns to wear. But no, she was surrounded by dirty dishes—in or out of the kitchen. One day, she would run away from Lord Tyalt's holdings and make a new life for herself—an exciting life!

First, she would have to come up with a plan.

"Hey, girl."

Madla turned and found Lord Tyalt looking at her. Her face felt hot, and her palms clammy.

"Yes, you. Come here," he ordered.

He smiled at her. She discarded the dirty cloth and attempted to smooth out her crumpled gown, cursing the gravy stains. She quickly pinched her cheeks to make them rosy. Holding her head high, she swaggered over to him. Perhaps he liked what he saw, and maybe this would be the start of the plan she needed. She walked up to the table and smiled down at him.

"Yes, me Lord," she said in her most posh voice. "You wish ta speak ta me?"

Lord Tyalt's eyes were bright, and his smile wide. Madla felt a stirring in her stomach and lowered her eyes. He was so handsome, he could not possibly desire her. Could he? Heat washed over her body, and natural colour rushed to her cheeks.

"Yes, I want you to fetch something for me," said Lord Tyalt.

His voice was sweet to her ears. "Of course, me lord."

She would do anything for him. She knew what he planned. He would ask her to retrieve something from his chamber, and then he would follow her there. It would be so romantic, and she would leave the kitchen forever.

"There is a book in the library. I wish to show it to one of my guests," he informed her. "You will find it on the desk near the window. Please fetch it for me."

The library? Madla gazed at Lord Tyalt for a moment, feeling the colour drain from her face, but she quickly recovered. "Straight away, me lord," she said with a small curtsy.

He rewarded her with another bright smile. She turned and hurried from the great hall.

By the time Madla reached the library, she was angry. Fancy believing a great lord would want anything to do with a silly scullery maid.

Madla forgot her anger when she walked into the library. Large, leather-bound books lined bookcases that stretched across every wall from floor to ceiling. She ran her fingertips over the covers and picked up a book to stare at the words. If only she could read. Some of the books had diagrams. She found these ones especially fascinating and flipped reverently through the pages.

Eventually, Madla pulled herself out of the book she was looking at and ran to the desk under the window. The book she had been sent to retrieve was old and smelled of mould. She peeked inside to see if there were any pictures. There were. Lots of them. Her eyes widened at the scenes displayed before her.

She turned the page and saw a drawing of a huge dragon, its wings spread wide and fire coming from its mouth. A man with a sword stood staring up at the beast. Touching the page with her fingers, she traced the outline, her thoughts turning inward. When would she escape the world in which she lived? She thought about the adventure and excitement she would have and about how she would never wash another dish in her life.

"If only me life was diff'rent," she whispered.

The light in the room faded, and Madla panicked. How long had she been absorbed in the books? Lord Tyalt would be angry, and she might receive a flogging for not obeying his instructions. She turned, the book clasped tightly in her arms. She would run back to the great hall and make some excuse for being so long.

She remained still—everything had changed. There were no bookcases, no books, no furniture and no door. And no library! Her hands trembled. A cold draft swept around her shoulders as she hugged the book close to her breast.

Where am I?

The haze shifted, and Madla stared at the dark, stone walls of a tunnel. Without uttering a sound, she was drawn in the direction of the only light.

Her gown dragged along the dirt. She held the old, leather book against her body, straining to hear any noise other than the flicker of the torch she moved towards. Small shadows danced across the walls and ceiling, but she heard nothing.

Madla stared in both directions. Nothing. The feeble light did not help her see farther than the small circle of light she stood in. Reaching up, her fingers trembled as she yanked at the long handle of the torch. It came free with ease, and she sighed with relief. Holding it aloft, she crept along the tunnel.

The farther she walked, the more nervous she became. A tight knot developed in her stomach and her skin began to crawl. Finally, she saw another dim light in the distance.

Madla moved carefully towards it. Leaving the confines of the tunnel, she entered a cave. Dripping water echoed around her. Her flat shoes scraped on the dirt, and goosebumps spread up her arms. A noise startled her. She stopped walking and looked up. What was that? She took another step.

The space above her head vibrated. An eerie squeal and a flapping sound pierced the silence.

"Oh," she whispered.

A small, black creature swooped down. Followed by several others. Madla screamed. They whooshed past her head.

Heaving the book onto the top of her head, Madla ran. Bats screeched, swooped and flapped around her. As she neared the light, she saw two exits—a large stone door with a large handle and a cast-iron gate. The light shone from the other side of the gate. What if both exits are locked? What will I do? Waving the torch above her head, Madla ran up to the gate and threw her weight against it. It swung open, she fell through, and the gate slammed shut behind her. The bats flew back into the darkness and disappeared.

Madla lay sprawled on the ground for some time

while her heartbeat slowed and she thought about where she was. She stared at the gate; it was quiet on the other side now. Where was she? How did she get here, and how would she get back to the library? Perhaps she had found a secret passage in the castle, and this would be her way to freedom.

She rubbed the small lump on the back of her head and looked around. A tiny seed of a plan started to form in her mind. Find the exit and get out of the castle. Go to the nearest town. Find someone to remove the tattoo from her wrist, which marked her as the property of Lord Tyalt. Sitting up, she nodded and smiled with excitement. Yes, that was it, without the mark of ownership, she could flee her life of servitude. She would remove it herself if she had to.

And then she would be free.

Exhilarated, she clambered to her feet.

Brushing the dust from her dirty gown, Madla picked up the book and retrieved the torch. She would find the exit and make a new life for herself.

A glint of light got her attention. It came from beneath another torch fixed to the wall. On closer inspection, Madla discovered a small hole in the stone and within the confined space sat a white-handled dagger.

She stared at it for a moment. It might come in handy. Without a second thought, she grabbed it and put it in the pocket of her gown.

The previous feelings of fear gone, she walked faster than before, eager to find the way out. Unable to judge the passing of time, she did not know how long it was before she saw the next light.

Her pace quickened. She felt the air shift at the exact moment she left the tunnel and entered another cavern.

Weary of bats, she listened for the first signs of their attack.

Thud. Thud. Thud.

The sound was different. She knew it could not be bat wings. The hair on the back of her neck stood on end. She saw another gate and another stone door. Could she make it? Willing herself not to fall over, she walked faster.

Thud. Thud. Thud.

Despite the way her body betrayed her, Madla refused to panic. The gate was not far. She could make it.

Thud. Thud. Thud.

It came from both sides. Madla stumbled on the hem of her gown and almost dropped the book. Her heart beat loud and hard. She broke into a run, her eyes never leaving the gate.

Thud, thud. Thud, thud.

The gate was a few steps away. A smile touched her lips. She threw her shoulder against the gate and fell to the ground when the gate refused to budge.

"No," she cried. "It has gotta open."

The book and torch lay forgotten on the ground. Scrambling to her feet, she rattled the gate. Locked. She looked at the stone door, but there was not enough time to reach it.

Thud, thud. Thud, thud.

Bending to grab the torch, Madla drew the dagger from her skirt. Her breath came in short gasps. She swung from side to side in anguish. A deep growl and movement just outside the circle of light startled her. A flash of yellow eyes. Wolves.

"I ain't gonna hurt ya." She kept her voice low and

pressed her back to the gate once again, hoping it would open. It did not.

Silence. Sweat dribbled down her temples. "Where are ya?"

The wolves growled. Claws scraped the dry dirt as they jumped into the light. Madla screamed and waved the torch in front of her. The wolves disappeared into the darkness.

Madla staggered towards the stone door. The wolves padded silently behind her. Again, she forced her weight against the door, then grabbed the handle and pulled, but it refused to budge. Moaning in despair, she turned.

A wolf stood in the light, his head low to the ground and slobber dripping from long, eager fangs.

Madla heard a deep growl behind her and froze. Sounds of snapping jaws were quickly followed by a something crashing into her back. The impact of the heavy body caught her off guard, and sent her tumbling to the ground. Razor-sharp teeth ripped through the skirt of her gown. Madla swung the dagger in one swift movement—its point found the wolf's flesh. Warm blood spurted from the deep wound. Her bloody hand slipped from the handle of the dagger as the wolf wobbled and slumped to the ground.

Its mate howled!

Deep growls echoed around the cavern. The second wolf leapt. Madla twisted away, pushed herself to her feet, and retreated further into the cavern. The wolf pursued her, its paws visible at the edge of the torchlight.

Stay calm. Do not run. Think!

The wolf attacked again. Madla swung the torch at its

head, knocking it off its feet.

The dagger!

Madla returned to the first wolf and grabbed the white-handled dagger. As she wrenched it free, the animal yelped, then went still.

A chime sounded.

Madla gained her feet and swung around. A faint, blue light glowed beside the gate. What was it? Would it allow her to pass through the gate? Lifting the hem of her gown in one hand, she ran towards the blue glow.

Thud, thud.

"No!"

A small gold key glistened inside a clear stone below the blue light. Madla pounded the wall with her fist, but could not obtain the key.

"Why?"

A massive force smashed into her from behind. Her body crashed against the stone wall as sharp claws ripped open the skin on her arms. Tears blurred her vision. She twisted around and buried the dagger into the wolf's stomach. Warm drool splashed across her face, and rotten breath filled her nostrils. The wolf fell to the ground.

Madla grasped the dagger firmly in her hand and watched the animal. A realisation struck her. I have to kill it. To get the key, I have to kill the wolves! There was no going back, or forward, without the key. Without hesitation, she bent over and drove the dagger into the animal's back. The wolf gasped for air.

Tears spilled down Madla's face. She needed the key, and the wolf was suffering. She had never killed anything in her life; not even a chicken for Lord Tyalt's table.

"I am sorry," she whispered and plunged the dagger into the wounded animal's chest.

More blood darkened the soil.

"I do not wanna do it again," she sobbed, pulling the dagger free.

A chime sounded once more.

The wolf was dead. Madla wiped the tears from her face, her hands warm and sticky. She looked at her bloodied fingers and grimaced. Why is this happening? She stood up. Out of nowhere, a leather lead appeared beside the dead animal's body. Too exhausted to be surprised, Madla picked it up, then turned to peer at the key. It was hers.

Madla picked up the discarded torch, retrieved the book and went to the gate. The little gold key fit the mechanism. She opened the gate and tried to remove the key, but it remained firmly in place. She struggled for several heartbeats before deciding to leave it.

The gate snapped shut behind her. Curious, Madla turned and tried to open the gate, but it was once again locked. She reached through the bars and discovered the key gone. There was no going back; the only way was forward, into the unknown.

Madla put down her horde and sat on the ground. Her dress was splattered with blood, as were her hands and probably her face. She grabbed the ripped portion of her skirt and tore a piece off to wrap around her arm; it was bleeding but not enough to cause her concern. She tore another section off and wiped the blood from her face. A third piece was used to blow her nose.

Closing her eyes, she leaned her head against the cold stone wall and sighed. Gaining her freedom was not meant to be this hard. She did not think she would have to kill anything. How many more caverns and gates would she have to pass through before being free? *Should I try the stone door?* She shook her head. She could see what lay beyond the gate but feared what lay beyond the stone door.

Wiping the blood off the blade, Madla stared at the leather lead. It had appeared out of nowhere—was it magical? Placing the dagger into the pocket of her gown, she took the lead in her hands. It was two arms in length and had silver clasps at both ends. It did not look useful, yet she pushed it into her pocket and stood up. With a quick glance at the gate, Madla set off on the next part of her journey to freedom.

Madla dragged her feet. The tunnel went on forever. There was no sound, no movement and no light in the distance. She thought about her pallet in the castle's kitchen. Even her thin blanket would be welcomed now. She would reach for the cup she had salvaged from the pit, the one with the big chip in the rim and the broken handle, and she would sip the murky water. She ran her dry tongue over her cracked lips with longing. Cook would give her a thick slice of bread covered in dripping for breakfast. Her stomach growled with pleasure at the thought. Was it still night-time or had morning come and gone?

She continued walking.

The path turned abruptly, then turned again. Finally, a light appeared. Walking faster, Madla reached the next bend and paused. Is it the sun? Am I almost free? No, it was not natural light. Madla past through a low opening in the rocks and emerged into another cavern. This one twice the size of the others and well-lit.

A strong wind rushed around her, pulling at her hair and gown, forcing her to stand still for a moment to catch her breath. The torch flickered and died.

"Oh!"

The wind ceased instantly. Unnaturally. A knot tightened Madla's empty stomach.

Set into the rock on the far side of the cavern were the stone door and iron gate. Knowing both would be locked, she turned her attention to the other things of interest—two blue lights, about five-arm lengths apart.

Would it be that simple? No killing this time, just take the key and go?

Madla smiled. Breathing a sigh of relief, she walked in the direction of the closest blue light. There was no key. Below each light was a silver loop.

Confused, she checked the gate. It was locked; just as she had expected. Placing the book beside the gate, she tried to open the stone door, without success. What was she to do?

A rock skipped across the dirt, and her heart missed a beat in unison. She turned. Two black eyes glared at her from across the cavern. They were perched singularly on top of two scaly green heads which swayed back and forth as the creature they belonged to swung its vast body towards her. Silver-studded wrist bands glistened in the firelight as the creature heaved its mighty war hammer onto his broad shoulder.

Madla looked at the wooden torch and swallowed. It was no match for a war hammer, and she was no match for the creature.

"You ... kill ... wolves." The creature pointed at her. "Ral ... kill ... you!"

"I did not wanna," Madla pleaded. "I had no choice. I am sorry. Please let me pass."

Ral's feet thudded heavily in the dirt. Madla feared the creature did not understand her. She left the gate and ran. Ral followed. The cavern was large, and Ral moved much slower than Madla. Running from one spot to another, Madla managed to stay out of Ral's reach but for how long? How long would this gambit go on? She knew there was no turning back and no moving forward until she defeated this creature.

Anger filled her body and determination filled her mind. Ral would be stronger, but Madla was faster, and she would win. She had an advantage, and that gave her hope.

"I have ta fight!"

Madla swung around. Ral was ten paces away. She had to wound him—get him off his feet. Holding the unlit torch with both hands, Madla rushed at him. She swung the torch with all her strength. It crashed into Ral's leg. He roared, and Madla retreated out of reach.

Each time Ral drew close Madla ran at him and swung her torch. She repeatedly smashed her meagre weapon against the same leg, but Ral's step did not waver. He swung his hammer with force. Madla screamed and skirted out the way, and the war hammer landed heavily in the dirt. Before the dust settled, Ral heaved the hammer over his shoulder and closed in on Madla. She ran at him again, but this time she stayed clear of his weapon. She ran past him and attacked from behind then she rushed out of his grasp.

Breathless, she leaned against the wall and remembered the dagger. The ground rumbled as Ral ambled towards her. Taking deep breaths, Madla willed herself to focus and be quick-footed. She grasped the dagger tightly in her hand and waited.

When Ral was close enough, Madla attacked. Speed and agility were with her. Passing him then turning back, she drove the dagger into Ral's injured leg. With a gasp, she yanked it out and plunged it in deeper. Thick blood smothered her hand and oozed down his leg. With a quick slippery twist, she pulled it out a second time. Ral's roar echoed around the chamber, but he remained standing, and he swung his hammer again. A mighty blow struck Madla, sending her skidding across the dirt, the breath knocked out of her. There was no pain, yet, but thoughts of broken bones filled her mind.

Scrambling to her feet, she felt a hand grab her hair and haul her backwards. Pain shot through her body when she landed roughly on the ground. As she scuttled to her feet, her fingers touched the spot where long hair once grew. Blood smeared her fingertips. A sob caught in her throat as she limped away.

Angry, she thrust her hand into her pocket and took out the lead. Steadying herself, she chewed her lower lip and waited for Ral to approach. She bolted towards him again. This time she ran to the opposite side of his body and circled around him. Ral paused in confusion. Madla reached up and snapped the clasp onto Ral's wrist band; the hand that held the war hammer. Madla darted past him and ran to stand beneath one of the loops.

She waited for his advance.

He came close. Madla reached for the loose end of the lead and ran to the opposite loop, praying it would reach. Stretching up, she fitted the silver clasp in place, then scurried to safety and turned to see if her plan had worked.

Ral roared with anger, swinging the hammer against the cavern wall. Dust filled the air. He moved towards Madla, but the lead pulled tight. Ral bent his head back and let out a loud, terrifying cry. He dropped the war hammer and grabbed the lead. Madla's heart pounded as she strained to see if it would break under Ral's savage tugging. Her eyes on the discarded hammer, a new idea took hold. She crept forward. Her hand shook as her fingers closed around the handle, and she inched it away as quietly as she could, dragging it out of Ral's reach.

A bright, white light caught her attention. She looked up, the war hammer no longer a threat. The white light swirled around and around the lead, then shot into Ral's wrist band. He opened his mouth and screamed in agony. The source of her attention disappeared. Ral stood passive and still, the lead now a solid pole.

A chime sounded.

Madla slumped to her knees.

Images of the first wolf she had killed in the previous cavern crammed her mind, filling her with knowledge. A second magical lead would be beneath or near the animal's dead body. She knew it like she knew every inch of her mother's face. She should have checked. "I failed."

She did not know whether to laugh or cry. She had trapped Ral, but she needed the second lead to free the key. She was doomed!

Climbing to her feet, she left her things lying in the dirt and walked to stand in front of the blue light. As

56

expected, there it was, a small gold key. What Madla did not expect was that it was free for the taking. But she had not completed the challenge. Only one lead had been used, not two. Turning, her gaze found the war hammer. Maybe gaining possession of the weapon was the challenge. She shrugged. Did it matter? The key was free. With a sigh of relief, she took it and ran back to her few belongings. Not wanting to leave anything, she added the war hammer to her horde and staggered to the gate where she retrieved the book.

She pushed the key into the lock.

A moment later, the gate closed behind her and Madla sank to the ground in exhaustion.

Opening her eyes, Madla felt groggy and pushed the dream away. Lifting her head, she looked around and sighed with disappointment. She had slept, but it was not a dream. Everything was just how she left it—the gate, the lighted torch fastened to the wall, the discarded book and ... a sword!

Madla stood up and reached for the sheathed sword. The excitement of handling such a beautiful weapon was overshadowed by the fear of what was to come. What creature would she have to face with a sword? Where was the exit? Freedom was the only thing she longed for.

She strapped the belt to her waist and unsheathed the sword. Long and slender, it was not too heavy but awkward none the less. Stepping from foot to foot, she waved the sword in the air and groaned. The movement felt clumsy and ineffective. Sheathing the sword, she bent over to pick up the book. Why she lugged it this far, she did not know, but she would not leave it behind. She retrieved the dead torch and held it up to the flame of the lighted torch on the wall. The fire jumped gracefully from one to the other, and she turned, feeling ready for whatever was thrust upon her.

At the next bend, Madla spotted the next lighted area. Recognising a pattern, she knew in her heart she was not truly ready. Pausing, she looked back in the direction of the previous gate. The war hammer? What had happened to it? There was no point going back because she knew it was gone. Stabbing pain in her stomach announced her despair, and the trickle of sweat between her shoulder blades confirmed what she had never felt before—utter fear of the unknown.

Madla stepped into the cavern. The sound of her footsteps did not echo, and the gate and stone door were exactly where she expected them to be. Holding her torch high, she soon found the bars of the gate in front of her.

Locked. No surprises there, but she had to check. The stone door would not budge. Placing the book near the gate, Madla waited for the inevitable.

Nothing happened, at first. Then, the air stirred and the ground rumbled. Dust filtered from cracks in the walls. Terrified, Madla retreated until her back pressed against the gate. She fumbled in her pocket, seeking the protection of her trusty dagger.

The cavern lit up with a red glow. Madla screamed.

Standing on the other side of the cavern was a giant red-eyed, purple dragon. The red glow she had seen only a moment earlier was the hot flames gushing from its mouth.

Madla's breathing came in quick gulps as panic

rushed through her body, and smoke filled her nostrils. To leave the cavern, she must kill the dragon. Or, she could cower in a corner and wait for certain death.

Returning the dagger to her pocket, she unsheathed the sword. Holding the torch aloft, she steadied herself. If she were going to die, she would do so fighting.

Taking a deep breath, she bounded across the cavern until the dragon came into view. She faltered, her attention on its feet or paws—she did not know what to call them—but they had deadly claws protruding from them. She jerked the sword clumsily along the scales, but nothing happened. The dragon shifted its weight, turning towards her. She continued running, hoping to find the entrance to the tunnel that led back to the previous gate. It would provide her with shelter and safety and would give her time to think.

Halfway there, a whooshing sound followed by force so severe it took her breath away, hit Madla in the stomach. Thrown off her feet, she landed on her back. The side of the dragon loomed before her. Scrambling to her feet, Madla grabbed the sword from the ground and clasped it tightly in her hand. The torch had fallen out of reach. She had to retrieve it before she was left to fight in the dark.

Her fingers reached towards the handle, as the hair on her neck stood on end. Peering over her shoulder, she discovered the dragon standing over her. She saw the glint of red eyes and the point of sharp claws slashing through the air towards her.

Already bent over, Madla fell forward and let herself roll to one side, colliding with the cause of the blow to her stomach—the dragon's thick tail.

Resisting the temptation to drive her sword into the

flesh, she stood. No time to feel pain. Another red glow lit the cavern. Smoke filled the air. She could hear the dragon's talons ripping chunks of dirt from the ground as it raced towards her. She could smell the dragon as it came closer. Her feet worked automatically to keep out of harm's way. Hair clung to her face. Her breath hurt her chest.

Gushes of air pushed her forward, but she did not know the cause until she heard the spreading and flapping of wings. Flames licked the dirt behind her. Heat swept over her sweating, aching body.

Madla knew what she was going to do, but she needed the opportunity. More flames beat the ground behind her, and the sound of rustling scales told her how far away the dragon was. She stopped running and turned, keeping her eyes fixed on the reptilian face, scaled and glistening in the flickering light. The dragon's jaws opened wide. It inhaled. Madla thrust her sword deep into the dragon's throat. Yanking it out, Madla jumped to the right. The bolt of fire hit the dirt where she had been standing.

Impulsively, she darted back and thrust the sword into the dragon's throat again. Glimpsing a talon swishing at her, she dropped to the ground and rolled to one side. Scrambling to her feet, Madla rushed forward and pushed her sword into the wound again.

Another intake of breath. Madla felt a cold sinking in the pit of her stomach. Maybe her plan was not going to work? Perhaps she was not strong enough or would not have the endurance needed. She dived towards the dragon as another flash of flames hit the ground. Driving the long, sharp blade of the sword into the dragon's chest with both hands, Madla pushed her weight and strength into her arms. A grunt left her lips when she pulled the sword free and turned to run away.

The dragon tried to pull itself to its full height, but the stone ceiling of the cavern was too low, and the dragon's head bumped into the stone with considerable force. It staggered and stumbled but threw down another gush of flames. Madla dodged away from it but caught a whiff of singeing hair. A sharp claw scraped Madla's skin. Blood spurted from the wound and Madla screamed in agony. Clutching her arm, she scrambled away.

I will win this fight, her mind roared in defiance.

Madla dropped into a crouch and waited. The dragon's enormous body pounded the ground as it bounded towards her. Madla remained still; calculating the exact moment to act. With a scream of fury, she sprang up—the force of her movement and the weight of the dragon combining as she rammed the sword into the dragon's throat. She threw her whole weight against the handle, driving it as far as it would go. She twisted the sword one way, then the other, and yanked it out.

The dragon screeched and swayed backwards. Still not satisfied, Madla plunged the sword into the dragon's heart then dropped to her knees, pulling the hilt of the sword down with her. Blood gushed from the deep wound as the blade sliced through the soft scales, the tip causing more internal damage. Chips of stone exploded from the wall as the dragon fell against it. Its talons scraped deep grooves in the dirt as the dragon's massive body shifted and slid down the wall. A small flame escaped its mouth, then it lay still and quiet.

A chime sounded.

Madla's body shook with exhaustion as she stood

beside the dragon, waiting. She pushed wet clumps of hair from her eyes, not caring about the amount of blood covering her hands. If anything appeared near the dragon, she would be ready.

A small egg! Was this her reward, or did she need this to defeat the next creature? Picking it up, she discovered it was heavy and solid. She looked at it briefly then dropped it into her pocket.

Looking in the direction of the gate, Madla saw the expected blue light and gold key. Gathering her things, she stood in front of the cast-iron gate and paused.

The gate led to another tunnel and presumably another cavern but what was behind the stone door? Was that the door to freedom? Up until now, she had chosen the gate because she could see what lay beyond, whereas what lay beyond the stone door was unknown.

The gate or the door?

She leaned forward and placed the key into the lock of the stone door and stepped through the opening. A warm breeze enfolded her body. Clutching the book tightly, she blinked several times and looked around.

Shocked, she looked around the library. Bright sunlight shone through the windows. She stared at the old desk as disappointment washed over her body.

Dropping the book onto the desk, Madla slumped into the chair and threw her upper body over the tabletop. Head in her arms, she sobbed. After everything she had endured, she was back where she started.

"It was all for nofin'," she sobbed. "I shoulda gone through the gate."

When her tears dried, Madla stood and felt for the sword. It was gone, as was the dagger. Yet pain told her she still had the wound in her arm and a bald spot on her head.

Leaving the book on the desk, Madla left the library. She did not know what Lord Tyalt would do or say, and she did not care. She hurried to the kitchen, hoping to find some leftovers to fill her empty stomach.

Cook glared at her when she entered the steamy, hot kitchen. "Where ya been? You are filthy."

"Lord Tyalt—" Madla started.

Cook glared at her again. "I do not wanna hear. Get them there dishes done, girl, then get cleaned up."

"But I do not do dishes now. I tend tables."

Cook lifted an eyebrow. "Spend a night with Lord Tyalt, and ya think ya too good for dishes, huh. Wash 'em!"

That night the hook-nosed storyteller held the crowd in awe with another magnificent story. This time he told of a girl and her quest through a set of caves. "She was young and inexperienced," he announced. "She was not learned, but she was intelligent. She was not strong, but she was resourceful, so when the dragon appeared, she refused to be beaten." He snatched a candlestick. "She was relentless. She thrust her sword into the dragon's throat over and over again. This angered the dragon. Fire blazed from its mouth, but Malad was quick-footed. She darted to one side then reappeared to bury the sword deep within the dragon's flesh again." The storyteller thrust the candlestick into the air several times.

"When the dragon was dead, Malad was free to move through the gate."

He jumped from the table and landed nimbly on his

feet. The candlestick crashed to the ground and rolled away. "But this time she found herself wondering what could be found behind the stone door. Was it more creatures to fight or was it something more sinister?"

Total silence washed over the great hall as the storyteller paused. He turned around slowly, obviously enjoying the tension.

"Malad's journey had come to an end. She was free." The short man turned to stare into the crowd. "But she was not free in the way she had wanted. Malad had used her intelligence and reasoning throughout the night, but what she did not know was that had she chosen the gate over the stone door, the journey to freedom would have continued forever. Each cavern would have produced something more terrifying and deadly until eventually, she would have lost the battle and her life." The man turned again, and this time, his eyes seemed to fall on Madla. "Sometimes, what can be seen is not always a safe path. Sometimes, it is necessary to go into the unknown to gain the things we want the most. Awakening our mind can provide us with the answer we seek."

The great hall fell silent. The strange man's eyes met Lord Tyalt's. "'Tis another night and another meal is requested, my lord. My time here will end in three short days, and then I must move onto the next castle and share my stories with new people."

Lord Tyalt's eyes were ablaze with wonder. "You have earned every mouthful and more." His beaming smile announced he was pleased—very pleased. "Food. My guest is hungry, and we want food."

The kitchen staff jumped into action.

Madla stood transfixed near the door. The storyteller

had told *her* story to the people in the great hall. So Genard had been a real person! A lump formed in Madla's throat. Thrusting her hand into her pocket, she drew out a dirty cloth to wipe her nose. Within the folds of the fabric was an egg—her prize for defeating the dragon. Her eyes widened at the golden shine the well-lit chamber produced from the egg. It was heavy, and another look convinced her that what she held was solid gold.

Folding the cloth over it, Madla pushed it deep into her pocket and smiled. A new plan formed in her mind. This time, it would work, and she would gain her freedom.

A voice penetrated her thoughts. "Hey, girl."

Madla looked up. Lord Tyalt beckoned to a young serving girl. Those large brown eyes, that winning smile and handsome face would fool anyone—they had deceived her, but she was wiser now.

"There's a book in the library I wish to show to one of my guests," Lord Tyalt informed the girl. "You'll find it on the desk near the window. Please fetch it for me."

Amulet of Kemet

P haraoh Ptolemy barely glanced at the trembling slave, or the angry red welts forming on his naked flesh, as Vizier Kontah's whip repeatedly whistled through the hot air.

"Insolence," the vizier hissed, "will not be tolerated. Back to work!"

The slave scrambled to his feet, tottered for a second, and staggered to the excavation of the future sacred pool.

The incident forgotten in an instant, Ptolemy continued his stroll through the building site of the Serapeum of Alexandria. It would be the most magnificent temple of all time, and the largest. He could see it clearly in his mind—dozens of tall columns, gardens shaded with palms and filled with sweet-smelling flowers, a waterfall cascading into the sacred pool, a library filled with many papyrus scrolls, and of course, a giant statue of Serapis.

Out of breath, Ptolemy paused, his short-cropped hair clinging to the nape of his thick neck under the heavy khepresh. With little more than a half-finished subsidiary temple and the foundations and columns for the main temple, he impatiently stared at the spot where a large fountain and garden were planned. With a smile, he tilted the heka he carried downward. Dragging the hook slowly through the soil, he channelled a small amount of energy out of his body and through the object. Tiny shoots instantly sprang out of the dirt. The saplings continued to grow into dense green foliage and flowers of every colour. His smile broadened. Yes, the temple would look grander than anything built before.

He straightened and snapped his fingers. Kontah rushed forward, bowing his head in respect.

"Yes, Chosen of Ra?"

"I want plaques made and distributed throughout the main temple as it is being built."

"What is to be written on these plaques, Divine King?" asked Kontah.

"I want the inscriptions to be in Greek and hieroglyphs, and every one of them is to say that I, Ptolemy III Euergetes, King of Kemet, built the Serapeum. I want the plaques made of silver, gold, bronze, sun-dried Nile mud and opaque glass. Understood?"

"Yes, Great One," said Kontah. He immediately gave orders to one of the many architects standing nearby, their gaze fixed on the ground at Pharaoh's feet. The man turned and hurried away.

Ptolemy smiled and continued his stroll. All the world, for centuries to come, would know of his greatness. He would make sure of it. He deserved nothing less.

Around the next corner, he found a group of slaves struggling with a massive stone block. With a sigh, Ptolemy held the heka and nekhakha across his chest.

"Thank the gods, your king and protector is merciful and is willing to help pestilence such as yourselves."

He closed his eyes, allowing the warmth in his belly to swirl around and around. He gathered the energy and pulled it up through his torso and down his arms until small sparks flashed from the heka and nekhakha. The power forced itself through the two objects and darted as a bolt of blue light towards the stone block. The block shifted forward as if a thousand slaves had pushed against it at once.

"Much better," said Ptolemy.

The slaves sank to their knees in thanks, their faces touching the dirt.

"The Living Image of Amum's generosity has not finished the task, scum of Seth," said Kontah, raising his whip. "Get back to work before I have you impaled for laziness!"

They scurried to their feet and immediately set to work on the next block. Ptolemy turned, signalled for his carriage to be brought to him directly and climbed up into its cool interior.

Puffing with exertion, Ptolemy made his way across his chamber to a large balcony. He could see all of Alexandria, even the dark water of the ocean in the distance contrasting against the light blue sky overhead.

A flat circular disc, the depet, flew into view. Ptolemy glanced at its flawless silver body curiously. Since the death of his father ten years ago, he had been in contact with those who called themselves Peherty, travellers, yet he had never physically seen them. For many years, generations of kings had an understanding with the

Peherty. At first, Ptolemy saw the wisdom of this association and especially enjoyed the help they gave in building the temples and his own burial tomb. But since the death of his daughter, something nagged at him to be wary of them.

He longed to remove the heavy khepresh, his crown, but he required it for public appearances, and it was the only means of communication with Peherty, who would speak to no other but the king.

"I see you have more blocks for the temple," he said aloud.

A sequence of clicking noises commenced. Ptolemy understood this to be Peherty's natural speech and the khepresh translated the sounds for him. "They are for the monolithic statues of your gods," came the monotonic reply.

"Good." Ptolemy grinned. "What of the slaves?"

"They are implanted with the knowledge they require."

A sound made Ptolemy turn around. Berenice, his wife, stood in the doorway with their eldest son, Lemy. Berenice's kohl-rimmed eyes narrowed when she saw the khepresh.

Ptolemy turned his back on them. "What else do you do to the slaves?"

"What we do is beyond your understanding. No one is harmed. That should be your only worry."

Anger swept over Ptolemy's body. He did not like being told what he should be concerned about.

"Father, do not question them," said Lemy, now at his side. "They must not leave before I take the throne."

Ptolemy looked down at his son. Dark, curly hair framed a round face, much like his own. "I am king and whether they stay or go is my decision."

"We have an agreement," said Peherty. "You cannot break it. You need us. We help you with construction—"

"And you experiment on the slaves," snarled Ptolemy, heat rising to his chubby cheeks at what sounded like a threat. "So you need us. I know the terms of the agreement. I am the Light of Ra that shines upon all Kemet and will not be told what I can and cannot do!"

He yanked the khepresh off his head, shutting off continued communication, and threw it against the wall.

"Ptolemy," said Berenice, her face dark with worry beneath the black wig, "send them away. We do not need them. You have the magic of the heka and nekhakha to help us build the tombs. I can show you something—"

"No!" yelled Lemy. "You know nothing of politics, Mother. Stay out of this."

Ptolemy glared at his son. The young boy repeatedly showed signs of being a threat in the future. He would have to observe him and Peherty if he intended to keep the throne—and his life.

"Ptolemy, wake up."

He forced his eyes open but saw little in the darkness. "Berenice? Why are you waking me at this hour?"

"A child has been found dead," said Berenice.

"Children die all the time." His voice cracked slightly.

"This one is different," replied Berenice. "When you see her, you will understand why."

Ptolemy looked at his wife. Her dark hair held back from her face with a twist of threaded gold, she wore a semi-transparent linen robe sashed below the breasts.

He grumbled, pushed himself out of bed and grabbed a robe. Some minutes later she led him into the royal nursery. Nerves gripped the pit of his stomach—memories of another night. "Berenice?"

"Our children are fine, but your cousin has lost his daughter this night."

Ptolemy saw a small gathering of people by the flickering glow of a torch. He heard weeping as he followed his wife to the small bed. A lump formed in his throat when Ptolemy finally looked down at the innocent young face. He stared at the body in disbelief. She could have been sleeping, but the colour of her skin told him differently. His heart pounded in his ears as he saw another child on another night.

"My King," said Berenice, "look at her neck." She tenderly moved the child's face to one side.

Ptolemy leaned forward and gaped at the circular puncture mark in the side of her tiny neck, the skin around it dark and swollen. A chill flashed down his spine.

"But that looks like—" the lump threatened to choke him. "Mefkat."

"That is why I brought you here," replied Berenice. "You would not have listened to me unless you saw this for yourself. I must show you—"

"Supreme One," said the infant's mother, tears streaming down her pale face. "Please, you must use your power to bring my child back to me."

The woman dropped her face into her hands and sobbed.

Ptolemy stared at her. He could not bring the child back just as he had failed to save his own flesh and blood. He struggled to find control, to find strength.

"I cannot save her," he said and left the chamber.

Ptolemy leaned back in his chair and looked at his war advisor. Mont sat wide-eyed and speechless, still digesting Ptolemy's latest news.

"My Kemet," said Mont, finally finding his voice, "messengers have been known to accept bribes to give false information. Can we believe this news?"

"There is no denying it. Menouthis and Tekinoe have sent word that they too, lost infants recently. They describe the same—" The lump returned. "The same wound. I have sent word to Canopus and Herakleion for their confirmation."

He pushed himself out of the chair with a struggle and paced the floor. "Prepare the city for war at once. The agreement is broken."

Mont gasped. "Your armies, Divine One, I can send word at once—"

"You have until sunrise to ready the city. Go!"

Robbed of his desire to sleep, Ptolemy spent the rest of the night listening to the movement within the palace wondering what the Peherty were capable of. Could he and his men defeat an unknown force? The tip of his finger ran over the hooked handle of the heka, moving slowly over the blue copper bands before finding the beads on one of the strands of the nekhakha. Would his own power be strong enough to protect his kingdom?

As the first glow of the morning sun stretched over

Kemet, Ptolemy picked up his khepresh and placed it on his head.

"You broke the agreement. The experiments must stop immediately!"

He expected silence while they discussed their options, but their reply came immediately. "What of your temples and burial tomb? We will not help you unless you help us."

"I have spoken. The agreement is no more."

His heart pounding furiously in his chest, Ptolemy pulled the khepresh off his head and dropped it onto the floor beside his feet.

The golden disc on the side of the khepresh shone white, but he ignored the signal for communication.

A familiar humming sound forced him to reach for the khepresh, the heka and the nekhakha and make his way to the balcony. The depet hovered dangerously close to the palace.

Ptolemy adorned the khepresh, the golden vulture on its brow heavy.

"You make a mistake, Human," said Peherty. "We will destroy your city."

"So be it." Ptolemy hurled the khepresh into the corner.

The depet hovered for a moment longer. Then it rose higher into the sky, showing its underbelly before moving gracefully away from the palace. A white light appeared from the bottom of it, swirling round and round, growing in speed and brightness.

Sweat gathered between Ptolemy's shoulder blades. Startled, he jolted backwards as a blinding beam shot downwards and exploded in the city streets. Puffs of smoke enveloped the depet, where it hovered for a moment then flew away.

Ptolemy looked at the three people sitting around the table—his wife, his eldest son and his war advisor—but he remained silent.

"It is a warning, Great One," said Mont. "You must take heed, or they will destroy us all."

Lemy sat beside the advisor, nodding his head in agreement. "We must not make enemies of Peherty, Father. Allow them to resume their experiments. You should align yourself to them and use their strength to take over neighbouring lands."

"Lemy," replied Ptolemy, "such an alliance would make us the slaves."

"I do not care," shouted Lemy. "When I am Lord of all Kemet, I will align with Peherty and use it for my own advancement. I will kill anyone who gets in my way."

"Such vicious threats from one so young," growled Ptolemy. "Pray for wisdom, child, as that will be your means to advancement."

"Great One, what of the attack?" said Mont, he left the table and moved quickly to the window. "The Temple of Yamm collapsed, and everyone inside was killed."

"They will be avenged," announced Ptolemy.

"Do you have the strength to forestall them, My King?" asked Berenice.

"I will try."

"There is something you must see—"

"Great One, the depet returns," said Mont. "Perhaps you should listen to what they have to say."

Ptolemy rushed to the window. The depet hovered as before. "I have listened to them long enough. Now it is time to show them what the Chosen of Ra can do."

Grasping his heka and nekhakha tightly to his chest, he stepped out on to the balcony. This time he would be ready. Warmth filled his body. He jolted as the heat turned to a flow of current. He watched the swirling pink light as it deepened to a vibrant red. The current intensified. Sweat rolled down his temples. He felt his limbs shudder violently as he used all his strength to hold power back. He waited, the smell of singed hair filling his nostrils and his heart thumping wildly in his chest.

With an involuntary grunt, Ptolemy released his arms. The current crackled past the heka and nekhakha. At the same time, the depet emitted a crimson beam towards the ground. The two energies collided with a loud explosion that thundered through the sky, sending sparks in every direction.

Above the chaos, Ptolemy could hear the screams of his people. Exhausted, he focussed on the energy left in his gut, willing it to build up again. His body shook with such intensity that the taste of bile entered his throat. He swallowed and concentrated harder as his aching muscles jolted in periodic spasms.

He wondered how he stayed upright. He smelt the unnerving scent of molten metal. Beads of sweat covered his body, trickling down the crevices of his back and legs.

With a sudden intake of breath, he flung his arms outwards, enabling the tension to explode through both heka and nekhakha. Through stinging eyes, he saw current hit the depet with force enough to send it hurtling out of view.

Ptolemy felt his knees buckle before he slumped to

the floor.

Berenice (Mefkat)
daughter of
Ptolemy III Euregetes and Berenice II
Aged 1
Safe Passage

Ptolemy gazed at the stone set into the wall, the words blurred by tears of grief.

Had it really been three years since he had held his little Mefkat in his arms and kissed her tiny forehead? The ache in his heart still throbbed as strongly as the morning he had heard Berenice scream. He had found her weeping bitterly beside little Mefkat's cradle. His baby girl had gone to be with Mother Isis in the afterlife.

"Ptolemy?"

The gentle voice probed his thoughts.

"I thought I would find you here. Are you strong enough to be out of bed so soon?"

He turned to face Berenice. "I miss her so much."

"As do I," said Berenice, with tear-stained cheeks.

A tightness caught hold of Ptolemy's throat. He coughed and spun around, not wanting Berenice to see his pain and uncertainty. Inside, his emotions were confused. His head told him he could not fend off Peherty for long. Yet ... his heart suspected betrayal, and it screamed for revenge.

"I want to show you something. And this time, you must listen to me," said Berenice.

He allowed her to take his hand and guide him through the dimly lit palace into the great hall, then through a gap between the wall and a giant statue of Serapis.

As he squeezed his bulk between the two unforgiving surfaces, Berenice grabbed a bar and pulled down with all her weight. He heard a crunch followed by a scraping noise as the wall gave way and a hidden door slid open.

"By the gods—" breathed Ptolemy.

"Say nothing," Berenice whispered.

Grabbing a torch that adorned the base of Serapis, she retook his hand and guided him into a narrow passage. The door closed suddenly behind them.

Dust filled his nostrils and caught in his throat. They descended many stone steps before passing through another opening into a larger chamber. Sure-footed, Berenice rushed forward. He could tell she had been here numerous times. He heard some clunking sounds, and suddenly flames of light lashed out of small stone holders placed evenly around the perimeter.

Berenice grinned at him. "Look at this place. I tried to tell you about it so many times."

Ptolemy gazed at the myriad of hieroglyphs covering the walls. "I am sorry. I did not know."

She spun lightly on her heel. "Come, we do not have time to waste. I must show you the wall that will interest you the most."

"You have read all this?"

"I found this chamber shortly after our little Mefkat travelled to the afterlife." Berenice paused for the briefest moment, but Ptolemy knew she still struggled with her loss, their loss. "I have been studying the texts on the walls for many months. The dialects have changed over time, but I can tell you what message these walls share."

She stopped beside a wall filled with hieroglyphs. In the middle, set into the stone, was a golden amulet. It resembled the shape of a man, wearing a khepresh and a false beard. In one hand he held a heka and in the other a nekhakha. On his chest laid an amulet.

Ptolemy stared in disbelief at his wife. His mind filled with every time he had shunned, interrupted and rudely ignored her pleas. She had accused him of not listening in the past. Now, he would listen to everything she was about to say.

"The walls tell the history of Peherty. How they came here and why," she said. "They came from the stars centuries ago and have helped our people ever since. They did this for the same reasons they do it for us—the experiments."

Ptolemy watched as Berenice moved around the walls, stopping intermittently as she read passages of texts as guidance.

"It is a long story," she continued, "and I wish I had found it earlier because then we would still have our Mefkat." She paused and took a deep breath. "I will tell you everything I have learned, but for now, you need to know that Peherty is using us in ways they have not explained. They need us to survive. They need the human womb for fertilisation of their eggs. At twelve weeks, the eggs are removed from the women and placed in an incubator until they hatch ten months later."

He saw her place a hand on her belly, knowing she felt the same as any of the violated women under his rule.

Speechless, guilt seeped through Ptolemy's entire

body. He had subjected his people to this treatment when he made the agreement with Peherty.

"Past kings added their own experiences to what is happening," said Berenice. "All are identical." She paused. "However, one king discovered this." She pointed to the amulet.

"What is it?" asked Ptolemy.

"It is called Nefer Ka. Used with the other items depicted, it increases your magical powers, and it is written that Peherty cannot withstand that power. These walls also state that Peherty will not destroy us, because they need us more than we need them. Without us, they will perish."

His wife's words echoed in Ptolemy's mind. He might be strong enough to put an end to this abhorrent threat after all.

"Take the amulet," urged Berenice. "You can save our people with it."

With shaking hands, he reached towards the amulet and gasped with surprise when Nefer Ka came away from the wall and fell heavily into his palm.

Berenice hung the amulet around his neck and affixed the false beard. She lovingly placed the khepresh on his head before handing him the heka for one hand and the nekhakha for the other.

She kissed his cheek. "I trust you, My King," she whispered, before bowing and backing away.

Ptolemy turned and walked out onto the balcony. "Peherty."

"Have you changed your mind?" asked Peherty.

"No," replied Ptolemy. "Leave, or I will declare war."

"Father, do not be foolish!" said Lemy. "They must stay."

"Lemy," said Berenice, "do not question your father's judgement."

"Very well," said Peherty, ignoring his son. "War you shall have."

Ptolemy tightened his grip on the magical objects in his hands and waited. He expected the weapon of the depet to light up as it prepared to barrage his city, but no light appeared.

Behind him, he heard shuffling and banging sounds. "Lemy, no!" screamed Berenice.

"I must stop him!"

Ptolemy spun around. "Lemy, sit down!" The words left his mouth before he saw the look of pure hatred on his son's face. Berenice gripped Lemy's shoulders tightly while Mont barred access to his father.

"If I have to kill you," said Lemy, struggling to free himself. "I will."

Ptolemy saw the bronze dagger grasped tightly in Lemy's hand.

"You wicked traitor," spat Mont.

"No, wait!" said Ptolemy and turned back to the depet. "What have you done to my son?"

"He belongs to us," said the voice. "He has proven himself useful over the years. As the eldest son of the king, he has access to any part of the kingdom without question. He was especially useful on the night your daughter died."

Anger washed over Ptolemy, and a wave of sickness almost made him choke. He took a deep breath. *Focus. Keep your focus.* He closed his eyes. *Serapis, give me the strength and power to avenge my little Mefkat and protect my people.*

He opened his eyes and glared at the depet hovering over his city. He swallowed, tightening his grip on the objects in his hand. "Kem Ka!" he bellowed.

"He has the amulet—" a series of frantic clicking noises sounded through the khepresh before it went silent.

Pink light swirled around the bottom of the depet. Ptolemy felt the energy build-up within. The sky darkened as thick clouds rolled in from every direction. The wind whipped at his robe. His insides were in turmoil as the power continued to accumulate.

A scuffling sound penetrated his concentration. He heard a thud as something fell to the ground. "Lemy!" yelled Berenice. "Oh, my son, I am so sorry."

Part of him wanted to turn and check on his wife, but it was too late. His own magic and that of Nefer Ka became one.

The light beneath the depet turned red.

Ptolemy flung out his arms, releasing the energy coursing through his body into the heka and nekhakha. A bolt of blue shot upwards and crashed against the underside of the depet. It jolted, and the red light faltered as the energy subsided. A crimson flash burst downwards destroying the temple's pylon gateway.

The clouds swirled overhead. Ptolemy thought of lightning, and the sky lit up. He thought of thunder as a loud bang rattled the earth. *I can control the weather*, he thought.

Before he could turn his mind back to the energy source within his body, a beam of red shot towards the subsidiary temple ...

Ptolemy's hand shot forward, and like a whip, the

nekhakha cut through the air in front of him. The three strands lashed out. He watched in amazement as they disconnected from the handle, grew in enormous length and intercepted the bolt. He steadied himself as an explosion caused thousands of sparkles to rain upon the temple. When his gaze returned to the nekhakha, the three strands remained in place.

"Ptolemy! Watch out!"

Without thought, Ptolemy stepped sideways. He spun around and found Mont glaring at him. Kneeling on the floor beside the table, a tearful Berenice cradled her unconscious son in her arms.

"Stop!" said Mont.

Ptolemy lashed out with the back of his hand. The advisor stumbled in shock, holding his cheek. Swishing the heka downwards in one quick movement, Ptolemy imagined the blue copper bands coming away. Mont took several steps backwards as the bands linked his wrists together. One lash with the nekhakha saw the advisor flying across the room, the beaded strands wrapping themselves around and around his thin body and affixing him to a column.

Ptolemy's gaze swept back to the city, and he saw billowing black smoke. His mind saw torrents of rain and the heavens opened up and drenched the fires. In quick succession, he sent lightning bolts towards the depet. They struck from every angle.

Small square holes appeared around its perimeter as Peherty sent bolts down to destroy Alexandria.

Ptolemy released lash after lash of beaded-strands from the nekhakha as the energy pumped through his body. No longer having to wait, he released bolts relentlessly.

He felt a hand on his arm. He looked down and found Berenice standing beside him. "Stop this, Ptolemy. We need them."

Ptolemy stared into his wife's vacant eyes. "You do not mean that."

"I do," she replied, flashing the dagger in her hand.

"Berenice, you are stronger than them," he said. "You never wanted them here. Never."

Her grip tightened.

"Think of our Mefkat and what they did to her."

Berenice doubled over as if in pain. She stumbled backwards and fell against the stone wall. "Ptolemy?" she whispered.

"Fight it, Berenice."

She groaned and fell to her knees, her hands clasping her head. "Leave me—" she screamed, "alone."

Ptolemy rushed to her side. "Berenice?"

Tears streamed down her face, but she pointed to the balcony. "Get rid of those sons of Seth for good."

He touched her hair and returned to the balcony. *For little Mefkat, for Berenice, for Lemy, for the people of Alexandria, and for Serapis, I will endure.*

Ptolemy straightened his back and gathered the energy within. "Kem Ka!"

The words echoed around the room and across the city. Numerous bolts of lightning struck the depet in unison.

Once again, a light flashed beneath the depet, deepening into a multitude of colours converging into a spinning vortex. The humming sound grew louder, and the wind generated by the depet more severe.

The energy within Ptolemy warmed his skin, tingled down his arms, sending sparks from the heka and nekhakha.

The rainbow-coloured lights spun faster and faster, causing the depet to visually vibrate.

The noise threatened to burst his eardrums. He crossed the heka and nekhakha on his chest, the amulet sitting just above them. "Serapis, do not desert me now."

He flung out his left hand in a sweeping motion, releasing the beaded strands from the nekhakha. Then his right hand, holding the heka, flew upward and over in a wide arc. A shimmering haze appeared over the city, stopping the violent wind immediately and cutting off all sound.

A rainbow-coloured bolt shot downwards at many different angles.

Ptolemy gulped, his gaze never leaving the multitude of colour, and then a feeling of joy filled his heart as the bolts reflected off the protective shield. Merging into one massive stream of bubbling light, it shot off in another direction leaving Alexandria unscathed.

Again, Ptolemy pushed lightning strikes and energy bolts directly at the weapon of the depet.

The depet rose into the air and disappeared through the dark clouds.

Ptolemy stood rigid, waiting and listening. Minutes passed. No attack came. Frustrated at not being able to see anything because of the dark clouds, he commanded them gone.

A smile touched his lips when he found himself gazing at his city. A perfect blue sky spanned above. Nothing spoiled the view. Not even the object that had been visible every day of his life, and for generations before that.

The depet was gone.

Two days later, Ptolemy looked up and found Mont hovering in the doorway. "What is it, Advisor?"

"Supreme One, a messenger has arrived from Menouthis," said Mont, his gaze fixed to the ground at Ptolemy's feet.

"What news?"

"The deflected bolt from the depet struck Tekinoe. The city sank into the sea. There are no survivors."

Ptolemy felt Berenice's hand tighten on his arm.

"Menouthis and Herakleion have major damage. It is unknown how many lives have been lost," concluded Mont.

"Prepare an escort," said Ptolemy. "At first light, we will travel to the affected area and attend the funeral of those lost. The cities will be rebuilt. I will place the first stone with Serapis' blessing."

"Yes, Great One," said Mont. He bowed and left the room.

"Oh, Ptolemy, a whole city and its people gone," said Berenice.

"Better a city sink than all of Kemet and its people obliterated, my dear," replied Ptolemy.

She nodded, her face white. "Can we trust Mont?"

"Yes. Peherty controlled his mind like they tried to control yours. He is himself now, but I am not so sure about Lemy." Ptolemy reached for his khepresh. "The job of rebuilding the cities will be easier now that I have the amulet, but I fear what might happen if it falls into the wrong hands. I have decided to return it to the secret chamber upon my return. Lemy will not be told about the chamber."

Berenice nodded.

Ptolemy squeezed her hand and left his chair. "I will walk the streets of Alexandria to see if anything needs urgent attention." The moment before he placed the khepresh on his head, he saw the golden disc suddenly flash white.

"We will return, more people will die, and your cities will crumble into the sea. You are but one king. Your son, the king after him and many future kings will do our bidding. We will never leave your world."

Boundaries

The open gash in my arm hurt beyond reason, but it was the blood that worried me. There was so much of it. It oozed through my fingers and dripped onto the long blades of grass at my feet. My heart hammered in my chest, but I could not stop here. I'd come too far. It was dangerous, and the sweet-smelling blood would not help. It would lead Master, and his hounds, straight to me.

I peered quickly into the lengthening shadows of the tall trees and then ripped the coarse shirt from my thin body—it would catch the blood for a while. I shuddered, not only from the cold but from fear and exhaustion.

Rustling sounds reached me.

Shirt held tightly in one hand, blood flowing down the other, I ran. The hounds would find me anyway, and the blood only made their job easier. I had no plan, no weapon, no warm clothing. It was not my intention to run from Master when I accidentally broke the expensive vase. It was reflex. That moment of action would cost me dearly. I had seen stronger men than me flogged to death for far less a crime. What had I been thinking? Escaping had never been an option. I knew that. All slaves knew it. The curse of Thanatos would kill me if Master's hounds did not.

Please guide me, Kathon. I do not know what I will find beyond the next set of trees. Where is the boundary? The thought terrified me and praying to my goddess seemed right, given the circumstances. It was evident that I was doomed, but I would not give up, not now. All I could think of was freedom and finding my beloved Zara. I would believe in Kathon and hope for a miracle.

My soft, thin-leather foot wraps were made for indoors, not running through the forest. Pain from the cuts in the bottoms of my feet seared up my legs, but adrenaline kept me moving. My back stung from that first slash of Master's whip as it ripped open my skin, leaving me in agony. I had been lucky that time, and the pain served as a constant reminder of the proper flogging I would receive if I got caught.

One hundred lashes.

The moon was barely visible beyond the thick mass of clouds. A few spots of cold rain splashed against my burning back. I groaned inwardly because my senses told me it was not rain, it was sleet. That is all I needed, on top of everything else that had gone wrong—snow.

I smelled the dogs before I saw them. They were ahead of me, and Master would not be far behind them. For a fleeting second, I wondered how that could be, how could they be in front of me. Was I lost? Of course I was! I had no idea where I was going. I tried to change course, but it was too late. They were already barking and racing towards me.

The whip and the dogs were Master's favourite entertainment. Those dogs had mauled many a victim at Master's command. It did not matter that the person was often innocent of any wrong doing.

The barking ceased. Instead, I heard deep, threatening growls. I pushed my way through the trees. My skin crawled with terror. Fear of being caught. Fear of the cursed boundaries.

Sharp teeth clamped tightly onto my leg. Pain shot through me. I fell forward, the shirt tangling with the undergrowth. Fresh cuts stung my arms and chest. Twisting, my free foot connected with the dog's head but his vice-like jaws bit harder into my flesh. Blood, slobber and sleet intermingled. Refusing to scream, I kicked him again, and more pain assaulted me, but he refused to release his grip. The second dog viciously shook the discarded shirt back and forth, warm saliva spraying into the air, landing in blobs on my ice-cold skin.

"Heel!" Master's voice bellowed. The dogs retreated, sat and waited for their next command.

My heart sank.

Master looked down at my battered body and smiled. "Tarmon, I see you are determined, and I have been entertained by the events of the past few hours." He flashed his white teeth at me again, then continued. "However, you will die from your wounds, from the cold," he shrugged and shot a crooked grin at the man standing in the shadows, "or, if luck prevails, the all-powerful Thanatos will poison your markings before the sun comes up."

The god of darkness, of death!

"Kathon, protect me," I whispered.

Master laughed. "Your Goddess will not protect you. You will be dead by morning."

My hand clawed at the damp earth. "I am your servant, Kathron. Please protect me."

Anger contorted Master's face. His whip sang through the air; the tip kissed my hand. My body twitched in agony, and sticky warmth flowed through my trembling fingers to mingle with the fertile earth.

"Go," Master bellowed, "but be warned, the game is not over. I will send men with hounds at dawn. If you live, they will end your suffering. Either way, they will drag your body back so that I can make an example of you in front of the other slaves. Insolence will not be tolerated."

I blinked in disbelief. My master said I could go. Stand and walk away. For a moment, I thought I was delusional. He was setting me free. It was a possibility that I had often dreamt about, but never in my entire life did I think it would come true. Our eyes locked again. When had I grown so defiant? Slaves never made eye contact with their masters. I heaved myself to my feet, wary of the dogs sitting close by. I would not give Master time to change his mind. Tearing my gaze away from the glint in his eyes, I turned and limped into the night. When I could no longer hear Master's deep, sardonic laugh, I collapsed to the ground and could not stop my body from shaking.

I do not think I was there for long. It was freezing. I wore no shirt, and my breeches were soaked right through, and I could feel my muscles reacting to the cold. My mind told me to get up and keep moving. I had been set free from a life of slavery. The thought terrified me, yet made me giddy with happiness too. Uneducated I might be, but everyone knew Freeman could move freely wherever they wanted, they made their own choices, and they had no reason to fear boundaries. There would be no more mending posh clothes while wearing rags myself. No more preparing scented, hot baths for Master then washing the grime from my own body using a stone and cold water from a jug. I would never sleep on a straw pallet in a tiny cupboard next to Master's room again. And there would be no more back-handers across the face, for no reason, when Master was in a mood. This was not the time to give up and die in the cold. Master had said I could go. I had no idea where I would go or what I would do, but I was free. I could choose to live or to die. That was enough to make me move.

I wanted life!

Life as a Freeman. A life I carved for myself. A life with Zara! I struggled to my feet and staggered on.

Pain seized me. Paralysed, I stood rigid as the pain increased. The night somehow turned into day. Or had it? I was not sure what was happening. I was not surprised to hear Master cackle and knew he stood behind me, watching.

He was not alone.

"Shall I stop now?" The voice belonged to Garde, Master's mage.

"No," Master replied. "I have always wanted to see what would happen. It was the reason I let him go. Your boundaries work well."

"Did you doubt them?"

"Not really."

"If I do not stop this now, it will kill him."

"I know." There was a pause. "Come. I will send men to bring back his corpse in the morning."

They must have walked away because their voices faded. Heat filled my stomach, and I could smell something burning. Was it me? I screamed. My skin crawled, my nostrils flared, and the pain and heat in my stomach increased. Still, I could not move. My throat rasped, and I realised that screaming was not helping. I needed to think. I needed to free myself. What held me, I did not know, but I knew that if I did not break free of it, I would die a horrible death.

Zara's sweet face filled my mind. Our love for each other had been doomed from that first moment our eyes locked. It was forbidden. We knew that. We should have turned away from each other, but we did not. Now she was a prisoner in an underground pit, and I was burning to death. Fresh screams left my body, cries of anger and hatred, of years of oppression and abuse, but mostly of loss. I had to live. I craved to be free. Besides, I loved her, and freedom was the only option to save her.

My skin tingled, my stomach was on fire. Strength erupted through the pain and anger. My teeth gritted together as I struggled.

Kathron, I beg you. I pushed with all my might.

The light snapped off, and I was surprised to find that it was still night as I stared briefly at the waning crescent moon. The burning sensation in my stomach ceased, but I could not move. A blue light burst into the night, dazzling me. The pain stopped abruptly, but my skin continued to smoulder.

My right foot moved forward, followed by my left. The blue light brightened to searing white, and I collapsed on the ground. Everything went black.

My eyes flickered open to find sunlight filtering through a window just above me. Hurried thoughts rushed through my mind. Where was I? How did I get here? Was I still free? Then my thoughts turned to surprise at the lack of pain I felt. I gently lifted my upper body onto one elbow and looked down at the narrow, but comfortable, bed I lie on. The sun's warm rays settled on me, and I did not have to push back the blankets to know the puncture marks from Master's hound had been washed and wrapped in a clean cloth. The welts on my back felt cool and pain-free. My gaze settled on my hand, and I stared at the red mark caused by his whip. Shifting my weight, I reached with my other hand to gently trace the mark only to discover the area felt almost numb. I expected searing pain, but there was none.

My gaze lifted. The room held little furniture. Next to the bed sat an old trunk. A table and chair filled the space beneath the window. Parchment and ink bottles littered the top of the table. Hanging from a hook on the back of the door was a long, black cloak.

Where am I?

My heartbeat quickened as I glanced at the door and then at the window. I figured that if the need arose, I could escape that way. It might be nailed shut! I stared at the frame and breathed a sigh of relief to see it latched but not permanently fixed in place.

In the distance, baying hounds rang like bells in my brain, and the log walls closed in on me. I left the bed and rushed to the door, feeling the soreness in my feet for the first time. Relief flooded me when the door opened into a bright, warm room.

"Ah, you wake at last." A man sat at a large, wooden desk covered with scrolls, quills and more ink.

I stepped into the room, my sore feet unable to enjoy the soft, woven carpet. Two questions ran through my mind. What happened? Why did only my feet hurt after everything Master had done to me?

"I thought it might be necessary to throw a bucket of water over you." The man laughed heartily, his bright blue eyes staring at me. "Do you have a name?"

As I nodded, my gaze roamed slowly around the room. Jars, stones, plants and scrolls covered the benches and shelves. Strange gadgets I could not name were piled in the corner. Against one wall, an open fire licked gently at a hanging pot, filling the room with warmth and cooking aromas. The room felt cosy in a messy but comfortable way. My attention returned to the old man. He was staring at me over thin glasses, a slight grin on his face.

"Tarmon," I blurted. "My name is Tarmon."

He nodded and lowered his gaze, and the quill in his hand continued to scribble something on a piece of parchment. "Well, Tarmon, there is porridge in the pot on the hook, if you want it, and fresh tea in the kettle."

Bewildered, I stared at the old man, wondering why he treated me like an equal. Or perhaps he planned to make me his slave. The cosy room seemed smaller somehow at the thought. Could I trust him? Should I? I looked at the unbarred door only a dozen steps away and cursed my lack of foresight as I thought of the latched window in the room behind me. I should have unlatched it to make escape easier. Would Master appear in the doorway? Had the man sent a message for him to come and collect me? Perhaps he expected a hefty reward for my capture. If that were so, the baying I could hear only minutes ago would be louder, but it was now only a faint sound in the distance.

I glanced at the man sitting at the table. He continued

to scribble on his parchment as I turned to the fireplace and scooped some porridge into a bowl. Tea, I had served it plenty of times, but never drank it. I poured some into a cup. I had questions, but I would have my fill first. It would give me strength, and I may not be offered another meal for a long time. My future was uncertain. I would eat, but I would remain watchful.

Out of habit, I ignored an empty chair and sat on a pile of old leather books to silently devour the sweet porridge. It was delicious, and I was as hungry as a wolf. The room was quiet, and the sound of the hounds suddenly grew louder, and that made me uneasy. "Where am I?"

"You are safe," the man replied. "They will not find you here."

My eyes narrowed. "Who are you, and how do you know?"

His eyes lifted from the parchment to stare at me. This time he was not smiling, and it made a shiver slither up my spine. "My name is Mak," he said, "and this is my home."

Holding his gaze, I felt a rush of heat in my cheeks, while my heart pounded savagely in my chest as I looked at Mak's unsmiling face. Was he angry? Would he strike me? "How do you know I am safe?"

To my relief, he smiled again. It touched his eyes, and I relaxed a little. "You have left the holding. They will not cross the boundary to look for you because they will not expect you to be able to cross it." He dabbed the nib on a dirty cloth, and then placed the quill and the scroll in a drawer. "No one crosses the boundary and lives. Except you, it seems."

"I crossed the boundary?" I felt the blood drain from

my face.

"Of course," replied Mak. "At first, I thought you were dead—"

"I am Branded." I automatically lifted a hand to touch the black tattoo on my shoulder. It had been etched in my first summer after birth. All my family and friends carried the same symbol. Only some had blue added to indicate they had been permitted to wed. Freeman called us Branded. We had no rights, no choices, no future. "It is impossible for Branded to cross the boundary. I know that. I witnessed what happens to Branded who do try to escape when I was a small child. The gate stood open, and a Branded man working close by saw an opportunity to escape. He rushed towards the gate and then froze. His body twitched, his skin—the smell gave me nightmares for months. Finally, he burst into flames and fell to the ground dead. I never thought of escape after seeing that."

I took a mouthful of tea. A horrid, bitter taste filled my mouth, and I pushed the cup away.

Mak stood and walked around the table, his long robe scraping softly on the carpet. "Next time, try stirring some sugar into it. It would taste better." He seated himself in the old chair across from me. "Mages use energy from beneath the ground to create magic. They spend their lives dedicated to their craft. Unfortunately, their talent is wasted in most cases, but there will come a day when things will change."

I was confused and a little offended. I could not read or write, but I was not stupid. "I know about mages. Garde is Master's mage. I never liked him. And I know about the boundary too. Thanatos cursed it. I should be dead if I attempted to cross it."

Mak laughed. "Your master wanted you to believe that story about the curse. It suited his needs. However, it is not a curse. The mage manipulates the energy within the ground. He wields it to do the master's bidding. It helps produce healthier crops in a good year or can save a failing crop in a bad year, but their main duty is to ensure Branded cannot cross the boundaries of the holding."

"How?"

"Your Brand is laced with magic," Mak replied. "If a slave tries to cross a boundary, the magic in the earth and the Brand amalgamate." He removed his spectacles and rubbed his eyes before perching the glasses on his nose again. He looked tired. "Unfortunately for the slave, the two are designed not to mix well, and the slave dies in agony, as you have already witnessed."

I blinked and stared into Mak's eyes. The room went quiet for several heartbeats.

Why did I live?

I would have asked him, but suddenly it did not seem important any more. I was alive and better still, free. I jumped to my feet. "Thank you, Kathon. I have left the holding. I will start a new life, a better life. I will make you proud. I promise." He paused. "But first I must save Zara!"

Mak insisted that I rest, so I spent the remainder of the day between sleeping, eating and planning. My appetite was enormous, and I ate anything offered to me. Sleeping, on the other hand, was difficult. I wanted to trust Mak but found one question kept nagging at me. *Why is he helping me?* I could think of no satisfactory reason so concentrated on putting a plan together instead. At best, my idea was vague. What did I know about life as a Freeman or about rescuing a slave from a protected holding? If I managed to save her, where would we go? How would we survive? I had nothing. No coins. No clothing. No food. Not even a blanket to keep us warm. Thoughts of fending for myself suddenly left me feeling anxious, yet looking after someone else as well made the fear intensify. My thoughts kept coming back to Mak. I toyed with the notion of slipping away in the night so that the old man did not know where I had gone. Maybe that would be the safest option. The more I thought about it, the more uncertain I became until eventually, I knew I could not start the new life I longed for without a little help.

"Tell me about Zara," said Mak, after the evening meal. He placed a pipe in his mouth and took several seconds to light it and then he drew in hard, a moment later, smoke poured from his nostrils. "How did you meet?"

It was a moment of decision for me. Mak had saved me, tended my wounds, and kept me safe all day. I could tell him nothing, slip away in the night and take my chances, or I could learn to trust, ask for his help and hope my trust was not misplaced.

"Zara and I are both personal servants," I replied, "and we met in town several months ago."

"Oh, you have left the holding then?" asked Mak.

I nodded. "Only to go into town with Master."

"Did you think of escaping then?"

My heart pounded in my chest. "Of course not! Master told me plainly that the curse of Thanatos would strike me down at dusk if I were not back on the holding."

"And you believed him?"

"Of course! I saw the body of his former servant. I knew it to be true."

Mak shook his head slowly and then drew on his pipe again. "Go on with your story."

"My master and her mistress sent us on errands and—" I lowered my eyes, my heart still pounded soundly in my ears, but this time for another reason, "—as soon as we saw each other, we fell in love."

My words did not express what I felt or the intensity of those first moments together. I looked up and found Mak smiling and nodding as if he understood.

"However, being servants from different holdings, we knew that we could never be together," I continued quickly before he could say anything, "and that our love was forbidden. We were lucky that Master and Mistress always went to town on the same day, so we were able to meet in secret for many, many weeks. We only spent a few minutes together, never longer, but then Mistress caught us."

Smoke swirled around Mak's head, but I hardly noticed. I stopped talking, remembering the look of horror on Zara's face and the look of anger on Mistress'. What happened then was a little blurry. "I remember pleading with Mistress and then promising that we would never see each other again. Each time I spoke, I made Mistress angrier—I remember seeing the veins in her neck protruding. That should have been my warning, but I could not stop myself. The whole time I talked, Zara cried openly. It tore at my heart, and then Mistress had struck Zara across the back with her silver-tipped cane, sending Zara to her hands and knees. Anger ruled me then. I ran up to Mistress and took both her arms in my hands, and I shook her. I am not sure what possessed me to do such a thing or what I said, and I was never sure who the screams belonged to—Zara, Mistress or me!"

I paused for a moment, breathless. "A stranger had intervened at that point. I found myself flat on my back, with a bloody nose and a cut cheek. The last I saw of Zara, she was being dragged away by Mistress, and I knew that she would be punished severely for what I had done."

"And you?"

"Beaten. Starved. Then put back to work," I replied. "But I was never taken to town again."

Mak shook his head in disbelief.

"Last week, Derk—he's the new slave who goes into town with Master—told me he heard Zara was locked in a pit with only crusts of bread to eat and some water to drink." I paused to steady myself. "It is my fault. I have to rescue her."

"Is that why you tried to escape yesterday?"

"Oh, no. I never intended to escape. It just happened. Master was bored, and I angered him by breaking something expensive, so he gave me several minutes head start and then let the hounds loose. It is a game he likes to play," I replied.

"And the wound on your back? How did that occur?"

"The tip of Master's whip caught me during the chase. Strangely, it gave me the strength I needed to keep going. Although he did find me again, and he let me go."

We were silent for a long time.

"I will help you rescue Zara," Mak announced through the smoke. "We will wait until tomorrow night. It will be safer because there will be a new moon."

Rested and well-fed, the hours passed slowly.

I could not see my back, but could not explain why there was no pain. I knew from experience that a whipping took a long time to heal.

I could see my other wounds. The bite on my leg was not as bad as I thought. There would be a large scar, but nothing more. Scabs had formed over the other cuts, and the bruising was already turning yellow.

I was amazed at how quickly the wounds were healing and considered myself lucky.

The outline of the new moon hovered almost unseen in the sky when we left the hut. A horrible chill pierced the woollen clothing Mak had given me, but there was no sign of snow. Anxiety gripped my innards straight away. The hut provided warmth and safety, but, outside, anything could happen. By the time we reached the tree line, panic had etched a deep fear into every fibre of my being.

"Mak, I do not know where Zara's holding is," I suddenly burst out. "What are we going to do? If we save her, how will I look after her, provide for her?"

"We will save her and then worry about that. I know where she is."

"You do? How?"

"The silver-tipped cane," Mak replied. "Only one woman owns a cane with that description."

A little further along, we came to a fork in the path. An old oak tree stood gravely at the junction, a wooden sign swinging gently in the breeze. "What does it say?" I asked.

"It is not important," replied Mak.

We took the right fork. We did not go far before we found ourselves standing within the shadows of another set of trees, staring at the holding. The main house stood tall and wide against a starless night, casting an ominous shadow across a winter field of wheat. Lights shone through the numerous windows and music drifted to our ears.

To the right, I saw the edge of building tucked behind the house. To the left, stood the stable. Even at this distance, I knew it to have white-washed walls and a thatched roof. Off to the side of the stable were several dozen small, rickety huts. No one had to tell me these were where the field servants and stablehands lived. The house servants would have pallets in the kitchen or storeroom, and the personal servants would have straw piled on a wooden cot or pallet in a small, windowless room next to their master's or mistress' chamber.

"Mak, where is the pit?" I whispered although I knew we were too far away for anyone to hear us.

Mak scanned the holding. He seemed to be looking for something. "It is over there," he pointed, but it was difficult to know where he meant, "behind the stable, to the side of where the servant's huts are."

I stared at him. "How do you know?"

"I have been here before." His white teeth gleamed for a second in the darkness. "I have seen it."

"Oh." An uneasy feeling stirred in the pit of my stomach.

"We must go now," Mak announced. He turned to look at me. "If we are caught, tell them you are with me."

Before I could ask what good that would do, Mak left the trees and followed the worn track down a slope and disappeared into the wheat field. I ran to catch up with him.

"Mak?"

"Not now," he said, placing one finger to his lips. "We must be quick and quiet."

Staring at his back, I followed silently. Stars twinkled above our heads, and the music grew louder as we approached the house. Stopping where the path continued up to the front door, we stared at the windows. Movement of the people inside. Laughter mingled with the music as it filtered towards us.

Trembling, I stared at the house. Mak turned to look at me. He put a finger to his lips again and pointed at the stables. I nodded. Mak did not run in that direction straight away, he placed a hand on my chest, and I felt a wave of warmth run through me. My fear subsided. A moment later, he turned and ran across the clearing.

Taking a deep breath, I stepped out of the shadows.

At that moment, the front door opened and light streamed from the interior. Rushing back into the wheat, I peered at the man standing just inside the door talking to someone I could not see.

Master!

The beat of my heart was loud. I was sure he heard it. Panic burned through me, my skin suddenly feeling hot beneath the unfamiliar fabric I wore. I pushed my way back into the wheat and moved slowly to the left, closer to where Mak had indicated. My stomach lurched with anxiety, yet I felt strangely in control as adrenaline pumped through my body. If Master saw me—my life would be over.

"Tarmon!"

Kathon, he has seen me. I stumbled, conflicting

thoughts surprising me. Run. Hide. Stand and fight. Grabbing the plants nearest me, I heaved my body through the gap and ran.

"Tarmon, over here."

It was not the expected roar of anger; it was a whisper of urgency. Mak. I turned and carelessly ran across the clearing. A single glance at the doorway showed Master, his back to me, as he continued his conversation. I fell to my knees beside the old man. There was great comfort in the strength of Mak's grip on my arm.

The murmur of Master's voice filled me with dread, almost crumbling my resolve.

Wasting no time, Mak rose to his feet and dragged me along behind him. Our backs pressed against the stone-slab wall of the house. We could hear the laughter from within and feel the rhythm of the music, which kept perfect time with my heartbeat. Before long, Mak halted, and I had my first view of the rear of the holding. More paddocks spread to the right. The building I had seen to the right of the house was not a building at all. Mesh cages as tall as a man ran the length of the scented garden located right behind the house. Dogs rested in those cages. How many I did not know, but thoughts of sharp teeth and claws pushed their way into my mind. I found myself touching the bite on my leg. I pulled my gaze away from the cages and looked at the tiny huts behind the stable. Row upon row, crammed close together, speckled the view. At that moment, I realised that all holdings were the same—they may have a different layout, but they were all oppressive. Never having set foot on another holding until then, I believed it was just my master's cruel mind that made our lives incredibly miserable. Maybe I was naïve, or perhaps I was indeed stupid after all, but it was a shock to find out that all slaves, everywhere, probably lived the life I knew. I took a deep breath and anger filled me, replacing the weak, fearful creature I had been all my life with a man bubbling with determination. *I will save Zara, and we will escape. Our children will be Freeman, not slaves.*

"Are you ready?" Mak pointed to the right of the stable. "We must go around them. The pit is located close to the huts, about three rows back, so we must be quiet. The Branded must not see us and raise the alarm. Do you understand?"

I nodded, but I did not understand. Why would the Branded raise the alarm? I felt that strange stirring in my stomach again, but I knew the answer. They think escape is impossible. If they did not raise the alarm, they would be punished in the harshest of ways.

"Come," said Mak.

We left the shadows and ran across the small clearing that served as a work area. Our feet thumped the hard-packed dirt. I worried we would alert everyone in the vicinity to our presence. A moment later, a head appeared over a stable half-door. My breath caught, but the curious horse munched his oats and watched without making a noise. My gaze flickered to a light that suddenly appeared in the groom's quarters at the other end of the stable block. Had we been heard? I ran faster. Mak veered to the right of the stable and ran across the grass towards Mistress' garden.

A dog barked.

Dropping to the ground, I strained my neck to see what was happening, but I could see neither dog nor people. The barking continued. Mak had not halted. He slowed, throwing an urgent look in my direction and kept running. On my feet in an instant, I chased after him.

By the time I reached Mak, he stood with a lighted torch in one hand. The flames licked the air, making shadows dance on the ground around his feet. Where did he get that? Something icy crawled up my spine. I began to ask about the torch, but let the question go when I saw the wooden grid. Below the slats, I saw the dirty face of a dark-haired woman cowering in the corner of the damp pit. Her large eyes stared at us, and her body shook.

"Zara!" I dropped to my knees, my hands gripping the wooden slats and pulling at them. They would not move.

"Tarmon!"

She scrambled to her feet, her filthy clothes hung in tatters from her shoulders. Cold fingers touched mine through the slats. A lump caught in my throat. In anger, I heaved on the slats again.

"I'll get you out," I promised even though the slats would not budge.

"Stand aside," Mak ordered. "Zara, cover your face."

Dogs barked again—more urgently now. I swung around, gazing intently at the dog cages. I watched them track back and forth behind the mesh, sniffing the air. They knew strangers were trespassing on their land. Alerted, their handlers left their quarters and ran towards the cages.

A flash of light illuminated us. I turned back to Mak. "We have been seen," I whispered.

"Help Zara out," Mak replied as if he had not heard what I said.

The wooden grid smouldered. How had that happened? What had Mak done? I glanced at Mak, but Zara reached up to me with long fingers, desperation on her face. Grabbing her hands, I pulled her up and out of the pit. She moved towards me. I wrapped my arms around her, pulling her close, brushing my lips against her hair. Even cold and dirty, she belonged in my embrace. It felt right, natural. Our hearts beat in unison. Despite everything, I could not stop a smile spreading across my face. I felt young and stupid. This was not the time to become love struck. My thoughts whirled, and I did not hear the words she spoke into my chest, I just felt her warm breath wash over me and held her tighter. I would never let her go.

"This way," Mak's voice broke the spell.

My focus zoomed out and away from Zara, and suddenly, the shouts of men up at the house reached me.

"The prisoner escapes!"

"Tarmon?" Zara trembled as her gaze settled on Mak. "This is madness. We cannot escape."

Mak grabbed my arm. "Follow me," he hissed. "Now!"

He ran between the rows of huts. Already, doors were opening, and slaves were stepping into our path. I grabbed Zara's hand and pulled her along with me. "We will escape, but we must stay with Mak. He is our only hope."

"Zara? Zara!" An elderly woman lurched at me, her calloused hands clawing at my skin. "Leave our Zara alone."

"Let me go, Mama," replied Zara, her pace not faltering.

Other slaves stood sleepy-eyed, watching without

knowing what they were seeing.

"You will get her killed! Do you hear me? Killed!" the woman yelled. "Zara, come back! Stop him!"

The Branded followed us. They tugged at Zara, they grabbed at me, trying to get me to release her. I never envisioned this, not for one second. I knew we had to outrun Mistress and Master, and their cronies, but I never thought I would have to fight off my own kind.

"Stop it," yelled Zara, tugging free from hands trying to restrain her. "I want to go."

"Go away!" I yelled as they swarmed around us. Clasping Zara's hand tightly, I willed her to run faster. I could already hear her gasping for breath. I scanned the people ahead of me. Mak? Without him, we would never find our way to freedom. I knew that now more than ever. I felt all hope recede and impending doom swallowing me whole.

"Leave me alone," Zara said to her people. "Let me go."

Branded continued to hinder us. They intended to stop our escape. They cared nothing for me, but they would not allow me to take their precious Zara to her death. How could they think such a thing? I loved her, and I meant to save her. They should be helping us.

I panicked.

A crack of lightning. A flash of light. Screams.

"Tarmon, oh, Tarmon," Zara yelled and stopped running. "They are dying."

My pace slowed to a stop. I felt overwhelmingly hot, and a searing noise filled my hearing. I turned to encourage Zara to keep moving, but instead, I felt a moment of horror. Fire, everywhere. Several Branded screamed in agony, flames mutilating their bodies. The stench of burning flesh intensified, forcing Zara to empty her stomach on the ground at our feet. Tears spilled down her face. I could not comfort her, could not move.

Unaffected Branded sidled away from us, running for cover, huddling together in fear.

I tasted bile in my throat. "If we stay, we are dead."

"I know," replied Zara.

"We cannot help them," I said and pulled on her arm, coaxing her to move away from the horrific scene.

"My family … and friends …" she sobbed, "are in pain."

I wanted to hold and comfort her then. I wanted to help these poor people. But there was no time, and we did not have the means. "We have to go."

A surge of relief swept through me when she pulled her gaze away from the burning people and continued running. I did not have to look at them to know their anguish, as we turned our backs on them and ran I heard their screams. I would have to live with the memory for the rest of my life. I did not plan this, but I was to blame for everything: their pain, their suffering and their deaths.

We finally reached the end of the row of huts, turned the corner and headed in the direction of the wheat field. As we ran, the Branded who lived in the unaffected rows of huts hovered together, staring at us, but none dared to venture near us. Screams and cries echoed in the night.

Finally, the wheat field came into view. I heard baying and knew Mistress had released the dogs. Time was running out. *Mak, where are you?*

"Tarmon, what are we to do?"

"We have to break the boundary," I replied. Even as the words tumbled from my mouth, doubts consumed me. The pain of that night was intense in my mind. I cursed myself for not asking Mak why I had survived. Could I endure it again? Could Zara? If caught, we would certainly die from the brutal flogging we were bound to receive, but, if we could not cross the boundary, then we would die anyway. I would no longer be content in a life of servitude now that I had dared to dream of freedom. It was clear to me that the only option was to try and escape.

We ran up the hill and into the trees. The dogs and their handlers were not far behind us.

"Tarmon, this way."

It was Mak. I was relieved to hear his voice, but my stomach turned over at the sound.

"Through here," he said.

We stumbled onto a worn path. A short distance away the oak tree with the wooden sign awaited, but we approached it from the opposite direction to the one we had taken earlier in the evening. I allowed myself to believe we might make it but as soon as the thought forced its way into my mind Master stepped out of the trees to stand in front of us. Then I glimpsed the silver-tipped cane and Mistress stepped on to the pathway too.

Zara sidled up to me. Her body shook uncontrollably.

I squeezed her hand but felt my own fingers tremble. Master's black glare pushed what little hope I had away. I could not pull my gaze from his. I could not block out the fading screams still floating on the night breeze, reminding me of the pain and suffering I had caused this night. Everything I had hoped for, gone. Master had won. He would rip Zara away from me and then gleefully take my life too. And I would welcome it because I would not endure my past life any longer.

"Mak, you caught them," Master said matter-of-factly.

I swung around to glare at Mak. The old man shook his head, and his eyes bore into mine.

"I will take my slave and will leave you now," added Master.

"No," Mistress stepped forward, "he broke through your mage's boundary and is on my holding. He rightfully belongs to me now."

I realised I was holding my breath, waiting for Master's reaction. For a moment, I thought he would turn and walk away. I glanced around, wondering if my life might be better on Mistress' holding. The terror in Zara's eyes told me it would not.

"No!" Master's hand grabbed my arm and tugged me in his direction.

Zara screamed. I glanced over my shoulder. Mistress held Zara tightly by the hair, but Zara still clung to me, refusing to let go. Mistress raised her cane and struck out. The crack of the cane against Zara's skull echoed in the night. Blood streamed down her pale face, and she fell to her knees beside me. The sound sickened me, but the blood did something else, it strengthened me.

"Do not do it, Tarmon," yelled Mak.

He had betrayed me. I did not care what he thought. Without warning, I yanked my arm free of Master's grip and swung my fist in the half-circle it took for me to face Mistress. The motion of my body combined with the anger I carried to the very core of my being sent Mistress a full two strides backward to land heavily on her back.

"Attack!" screamed the dog handlers.

The animals rushed towards me, saliva landing everywhere and growls drowning out the groans of Mistress.

My life was over. I had nothing more to lose.

"Stop! Stop this right now," demanded Mak.

I would not stop. I would die trying to protect Zara rather than be dragged back to Master's holding and flogged to death. I grabbed the silver-tipped cane from the ground. Four sets of jaws snapped at the air around me. I swung the cane from side to side. It whooshed through the air. I heard the grunts I made but felt disconnected from them somehow. One of the dogs sunk his teeth into the cloth of my breeches, and the seams ripped. The cane smashed down on his back. He let go of the fabric and yelped. I did not stop. The cane connected with his back again and again, and then I turned on another dog. My body tingled from the strain. Suddenly fire burst out from somewhere near me, licking at the dogs, singeing their fur. I rushed at them again, and more flames claimed the dog nearest to me. The dog's yelps rose into the night, causing the other dogs, and their handlers, to turn and disappear into the trees.

Sweat from the exertion streamed down my temples and between my shoulder blades. I spun around and froze.

Master had Zara pressed up against him. He used her body as a human shield.

"Well, that was quite a display," said Master.

I stood staring at him. His voice radiated confidence, yet fear flickered in his eyes. It gave me much satisfaction, even if I did not truly understand the reason why.

"Let her go!" I took a step closer.

Master dragged Zara backwards. "Will you kill her too?"

"Kill?" I faltered. "I have killed no one."

"I disagree," replied Master. "Think about it."

I felt the heat rushing through my body still. It travelled through my veins, making my fingertips tingle.

A hand pressed my arm. "Tarmon."

I glanced at Mak. "Get away from me. I trusted you, and you betrayed me."

"Let me explain—"

"I should have known when you knew where the pit was and when you said the slaves should not see us. My gut tried to warn me, but—"

"Listen to what I have to say—"

"I am through listening," I replied and turned my attention back to Master. "Let her go."

Then I saw the glint of a blade. One arm held Zara firmly around the throat, while the other held the point of a dagger to her side. She stood rigid in his grasp—her eyes glistening with fear, pleading for help.

"Let us go," I whispered.

Master threw back his head and laughed. "Never."

I felt the heat of anger ebb away, and then another movement made me turn away.

Mistress staggered towards us. "She is my slave. Give her to me."

Mistress reached for Zara. Zara struggled in Master's clutches, and I rushed forward. The dagger sunk into Zara's side. Her eyes fluttered closed as she crumpled to the ground, blood soaking her garment.

"Zara!"

My hands grabbed Mistress and flung her to one side. A heartbeat later, I stepped over Zara and my fist connected with Master's jaw. I heard the loud crack as his jaw dislocated. He stumbled sideways and then turned his bloody mouth towards me, sneering.

"I should have killed you myself," he said between clenched teeth, spitting blood.

"Now it is too late," I replied.

My fist connected again, and he staggered backwards. I stepped forward, my fist finding its target once more. I drew in a deep breath, held it, and threw my entire weight behind yet one last punch. Blood splattered my face, as Master fell backward, his head smashing against a tree trunk. He slid down to the ground and lay unmoving in the tall grass.

"Tarmon, enough!"

I spun on Mak, not caring if Master lived or died.

Mak stood passive, looking old and tired, and the energy motivating me slipped away. I rushed to Zara, who lay unmoving where she fell. Nearby, Mistress rolled onto her side but did not attempt to stand.

"I did not betray you," said Mak.

"You let me believe that I could rescue Zara and be free."

"Tarmon, you can never be free," Mak replied. "You are Branded, and that mark will never leave you."

"It could have," I yelled. "To be free, I would have cut it from my skin."

"The magic has entered your blood," Mak said softly. "You can never be free of it."

I stared at him, all hope lost, then turned my gaze to Zara.

"Every mage's boundary would have stopped you. Every holding you escaped would take you to another holding. You can never be free."

"You should have told me. Why did you let me put Zara's life at risk?" I was desperate to understand. "I thought there was a chance; otherwise, I would never have attempted to rescue her."

"I did not mean for things to turn out like this."

Mistress pulled herself up and got to her feet. "Grandfather, this is a common slave. You will not explain anything to him."

Grandfather? The remaining energy that possessed my body melted away. I blinked in shock.

"Ulmi—" said Mak.

"Do not call me that," yelled Mistress. "I have always hated it." She limped over at us and reached out a hand. "I will not allow you to have the girl."

"Touch her and I will kill you." The words slipped from my mouth like venom flies from a snake's fangs.

Mistress drew back her hand as if bitten. Her gaze went from Zara to me and then Mak.

Mak returned his granddaughter's gaze. "For years, I have allowed you free rein, but on this occasion, I will exert my authority. I have already penned the scroll. I am the master of this holding, and I claim Tarmon and Zara for myself."

"What!" I left Zara's side and faced Mak, grabbing the front of his cloak and dragging him towards me. "You would enslave me!"

"Get your hands off—" yelled Mistress, but Mak held up a hand and stopped the words in her mouth.

"Leave us! Now!" Mak glared at Mistress, and she turned and scurried away. Mak turned back to me. "No, I want to give you the freedom to do as you please. I wish to train you. I would like you to become my apprentice."

"Apprentice?"

"Yes, I am this holding's mage, and when I am gone, I would like you to take on the position."

I let go of Mak in disbelief. "You are a mage?"

"Yes," the old man replied. "How do you think your wounds healed so quickly?"

"I do not know. I was too busy planning Zara's rescue to think about it."

"Who do you think stopped the poison in your system when you ran into the boundary?" He did not pause. We stared at each other intently. "I knew you had the ability because you did not die instantly. Your body fought the power, but you were weak, so I helped you. At that moment, I chose you as my apprentice. I should have chosen someone years ago, but I have never found anyone worthy of the position. Your wish to save Zara was a noble one. Of course, I knew of her plight but had done nothing about it. Maybe I should have done. There are many things I should have done, but magic and its uses are my main focus. I have spent many years in this study. There is much that can be achieved with your ability, Tarmon."

"Yes, you should have helped her. Just like you should not have caused all that suffering back at the huts." My fist curled into a tight ball. "Why did you do that?"

"I did not," came Mak's reply. "You did."

"That is not true." I shook my head. I wanted to block out his words. He had to be wrong. Then I remembered that burning sensation in my stomach, the panic of being caught, the desire to break free from the crowd. Instinctively, I knew he was right. Shame consumed me.

"It was not intentional," said Mak, "but, you must learn to control it. I can teach you that. We will build a home for you and your family. You will be free to do as you please. You will have a life of freedom, even if you are not truly free. And we can study together, and we will find a way to change things. And the most important thing I can offer you is a promise that your children will never be Branded. The scroll I have prepared will ensure that."

"My children will be Freeman?"

"Yes, you have my word. Will you accept the position of my apprentice?"

I dreamed of freedom for Zara and me. I wanted our children to be Freeman. Tonight's outcome was not exactly what I had envisioned, but it was close. I knelt beside Zara and brushed strands of bloodied hair from her face. "Yes, I accept," I said as I gathered her into my arms.

Mak smiled and turned. He walked towards the oak tree, which marked the path to his hut. Holding my head high, I silently vowed to learn everything Mak was able to teach me and use that knowledge to change the lives of Branded forever.

About the Author

Born within the sound of the Bow bells in London, Karen Lee Field was seven when her parents decided to move to the "Lucky Country" and settle in Sydney, Australia. Apart from enjoying time with her family and pets, Karen loves escaping to fantasy worlds—places where her sometimes ordinary life is transformed into an exciting adventure and her imagination is set free. She writes novels for children and adults in various genres, and her short stories appear in several anthologies. She currently lives on the south coast of NSW.

www.karenleefield.com

Thanks for reading.

Please add a short review at the bookstore where you purchased this book, and let me know what you thought.

www.ingramcontent.com/pod-product-compliance
Lightning Source LLC
Chambersburg PA
CBHW071326130626
46556CB00004B/1764